The Wild One

ALSO BY RUTH CARDELLO

CORISI BILLIONAIRES

The Broken One

THE WESTERLYS

In the Heir
Up for Heir
Royal Heir
Hollywood Heir
Runaway Heir

LONE STAR BURN

Taken, Not Spurred
Tycoon Takedown
Taken Home
Taking Charge

THE LEGACY COLLECTION

Maid for the Billionaire
For Love or Legacy
Bedding the Billionaire
Saving the Sheikh
Rise of the Billionaire
Breaching the Billionaire: Alethea's Redemption
Recipe for Love (Holiday Novella)
A Corisi Christmas (Holiday Novella)

THE ANDRADES

Come Away with Me
Home to Me
Maximum Risk
Somewhere Along the Way
Loving Gigi

THE BARRINGTONS

Always Mine
Stolen Kisses
Trade It All
A Billionaire for Lexi
Let It Burn
More Than Love
Forever Now
Never Goodbye

TRILLIONAIRES

Prince Xander
Virgin for a Trillionaire

TEMPTATION SERIES

Twelve Days of Temptation
Be My Temptation

BACHELOR TOWER SERIES

Insatiable Bachelor
Impossible Bachelor
Undeniable Bachelor

The Wild One

RUTH CARDELLO

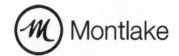 Montlake

Published by Montlake, Seattle

www.apub.com

Amazon, the Amazon logo, and Montlake are trademarks of Amazon.com, Inc., or its affiliates.

ISBN-13: 9781542017046
ISBN-10: 1542017041

Cover design by Eileen Carey

Printed in the United States of America

*This book is dedicated to my friend Erin.
Thank you for being so good to my family—those with
two legs as well as those with four. Your kindness to all
creatures is inspirational.*

—Ruthie

DON'T MISS A THING!

www.ruthcardello.com

Sign Up for Ruth's Newsletter
Yes, let's stay in touch!
https://forms.aweber.com/form/00/819443400.htm

Join Ruth's Private Fan Group
www.facebook.com/groups/ruthiesroadies

Follow Ruth on Goodreads
www.goodreads.com/author/show/4820876.
Ruth_Cardello

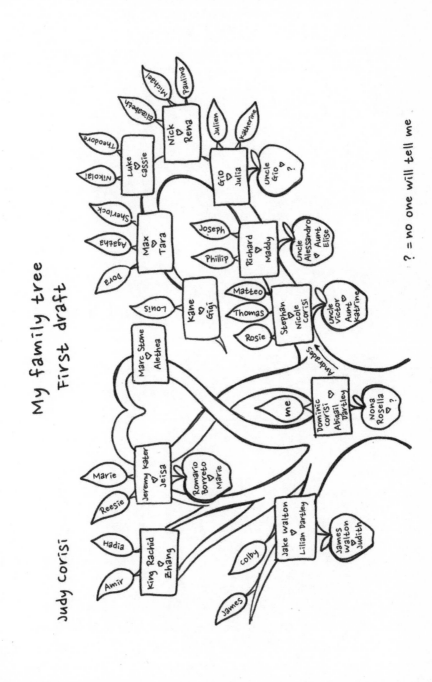

My family tree
First draft

Judy Corisi

? = no one will tell me

NOTE TO MY READERS

If you're discovering me through this series, you may come across some names you're not familiar with. These are Easter eggs, fun little finds, for readers who have been in my billionaire world since *Maid for the Billionaire*.

Dominic Corisi kicked off my career in 2011. He was how so many readers first found me, and he has remained a favorite for many. Although this book is primarily about Mauricio and Wren, the series is also about Dominic finally finding his family. It wouldn't be one of my romances if that was an easy journey.

Secrets can tear families apart, or they can heal them.

Some have to do one before they do the other.

So come meet Dominic for a second time and discover why.

CHAPTER ONE

JUDY CORISI'S FATHER, DOMINIC

Fresh from a meeting with the head of the Chinese division of his tech company, Dominic Corisi sat behind a large mahogany desk in his Upper Manhattan office. His phone beeped with a message from Jeremy Kater, one of his business partners: Meet me in WorkChat.

He replied via text without hesitation. No.

His phone rang a second later. "What do you have against WorkChat?" Jeremy asked in an amused tone.

"Besides the fact that you installed my competition's technology in my closet without my permission?"

"You're the one who says business is best done face-to-face. Plus, you know I modified it to meet our security needs."

"My issue with it isn't security related. Virtual reality is not face-to-face. And I don't care how you glorify holograms; I refuse to step into a closet to conduct business." Technology didn't intimidate Dominic. He'd built his fortune on it. No, the odd practices of the next generation did. Shortly after the install, he'd learned that one of his US-based team leaders had started using a filter that added a bunny face to Dominic when they spoke in WorkChat. Dominic brought that young man to his New York office to fire him in person, and he had yet to regret it. The man had shown up with a representative from human resources, like a child using a parent for protection. So Dominic had explained to both of them that real life doesn't have a filter. It was harsh, ugly, and often unforgiving.

I did that kid a favor. Weak never wins.

Coming back to the moment, Dominic inquired about Jeremy's wife. "How is Jeisa?"

"She's good. I thought she'd have more time now that Marie and Reesie are both in school, but she's even busier. Yoga. Soccer. Karate. Marie can already kick my ass."

"Not a difficult feat, I'm sure," Dominic joked, but there was no bite in his humor.

"So grumpy. Is it because you miss us?"

"That must be it," Dominic said in a dry tone. There was a time when he wouldn't have associated with someone like Jeremy. Despite the younger man's success, he remained eager to please and eternally optimistic. Dominic's childhood had left him too hardened to be able to stomach that type for long, but Jeremy was as loyal as he was brilliant. He'd earned his place at the table.

Loyalty made almost any sin pardonable.

Except fucking bunny ears.

Dominic's wife, Abby, had convinced him to rehire the young man and put him under Jake Walton's tutelage. Dominic didn't regret that either.

No one became one of the richest men in the world by playing nice, but for the past ten years, ever since Abigail Dartley had walked into his life and turned it upside down, Dominic had tried to be the man she deserved. Before her, he'd only known love to be fragile and angry—vindictive. That wasn't the way Abby loved. She'd raised her sister, Lil, after the death of their parents. She was strong, stable, infinitely patient. For her, love was a commitment . . . and a privilege. And he was a better man because of her.

Without her, vengeance had been his family.

She'd given him not only a daughter but also a second chance to be the brother to Nicole he always should have been. Without Abby, he would never have forgiven his mother.

His life was full of family—some by blood, many by choice.

A man like that was grateful enough to rehire someone he swore would never work for him again and not feel less for doing it. *I did make sure the kid left my office near tears and with a full understanding of what would happen if I heard he so much as whispered about why I'd fired him.*

Love had softened Dominic's heart, but he was still Dominic.

"Did you call for a reason?" Dominic prodded.

"Yes. This isn't an easy conversation for me—"

"Just say it. Did you crash a server? Violate a government treaty?" Whatever it was, there was a solution. Jeremy worried too much. Almost everything was fixable.

"It's about Judy."

Dominic tensed at the mention of his ten-year-old daughter. "What about her?" Nothing mattered to Dominic more than his wife and child. Not his business. Not his life. They were his Achilles' heel.

Jeremy continued, "I promised Judy I wouldn't say anything, but I have children, and if they were doing something like this . . . I'd want to know."

"Doing what?" Dominic growled the words between his clenched teeth.

"Don't get all worked up. It's not really bad. Well, it could be bad, but nothing has happened yet. And really, who knows, it might end up being a good thing in the end."

"Just tell me," Dominic roared.

"I feel guilty breaking Judy's confidence, but . . ."

"Oh my fucking God—"

"She asked me for help with a school assignment."

Jeremy's announcement circled in Dominic's head. He processed it through a filter of panic and fury. "If this is some kind of joke, I will kill you."

"She's working on a family tree for you as a surprise."

"What?"

"A family tree. You know—family, that thing you don't like to talk about? She wanted to add more branches to it and asked Alethea to help her discover more about your family."

Breathe. Don't punch the wall. Don't crush the phone. Breathe. "And that was difficult for you to tell me because?"

"Because Judy asked Alethea to help her first. Whatever Alethea found, she left no digital trace of it and told Judy she couldn't help her with it anymore."

"Sounds like a wise choice." Dominic walked to the large window of his office and stared out over the skyscrapers. He took another deep breath. Only a man with as many enemies as Dominic had would understand where his thoughts had taken him in the prior dark moments. *No one is in danger. Relax.* He knew his daughter had been assigned a family tree project the previous school year. She'd asked for his help with it, but there was a limit of what he wanted to remember . . . even for her. The past held too much pain.

Judy hadn't gotten a good grade on that assignment, and apparently that had bothered her enough to continue to work on it. *She's driven—like me.*

Dominic continued, "Now that you've started my day with a mild heart attack—"

"Sorry about that, but I'm concerned. Alethea doesn't stop. You know that. Once she starts digging, it's an addiction to her. She found something. I'd bet my life she did. Did she say anything to you?"

"No."

"See, that's what has me worried. I've retraced her online steps. Her search took her all the way to Italy. Then nothing. I don't like it. Alethea found something she couldn't tell you—couldn't tell Judy either. But what?"

"You're overthinking this. Alethea is a new mother. Her focus naturally switched to that over playing private eye."

"You're not curious about what she found? You might have family in Italy."

"I have all the family I need." The only peace Dominic found was by focusing on the present and those he loved today. The past only filled him with questions he couldn't answer. Extended family? Which side did he want to learn more about? His violent, abusive father's family? No. His mother's? Although she was back in his life and he'd forgiven her, she'd left her children when they'd most needed her, and they'd suffered for more than a decade . . . not knowing if she was dead or alive.

Did he need more like either of them in his life?

The answer was easy—hell no.

"What should I tell Judy?"

"I'll send you a few names to give her. Done." As calm returned, he added, "And thank you for bringing the matter to me. I won't betray your confidence to Judy. It's important for her to have people she feels she can turn to."

"We love her. We love you too. Anything you need. You know that, Dom."

"Okay. Tell Jeisa I said hello."

"I will. And you really don't want to know what Alethea found in Italy?"

"I really don't want to know. And if I ever do want to, I'll ask her."

"Sounds good. Hey, let's lighten the mood. I heard the funniest joke this morning. Want to hear it?"

Dominic ended the call without hesitation and pocketed his phone. He rubbed his chin and sighed. He'd have to say something to Abby about this. She wouldn't like that Judy was keeping secrets from them.

When it came to parenting, he and his wife often disagreed on how they saw situations. He'd learned, though, to discuss their differences in private and show only a united front to their daughter. In most cases, Dominic deferred to Abby when it came to doling out consequences.

Despite being ten, Judy would always be his little princess.

Proof that the world was capable of good.

His little angel had convinced one of his security team, Alethea, to conduct a covert operation they both knew he wouldn't approve of.

And when Alethea had failed to produce results . . . had Judy let that stop her? No. Instead, she'd contacted one of the world's most talented hackers and enlisted his help.

Dominic smiled.

That's my little girl.

CHAPTER TWO

MAURICIO

A major life crossroads—I found myself at one again.

This time, however, my path forward was less clear.

Returning to Paris had been a mistake. The city was full of fun, wild memories for me, but none that fit with the man I'd become. It was also frustrating as hell that the friend who had asked me for help was completely ghosting me.

"Felix didn't make our meeting," I said into my phone, not even attempting to hide my irritation. My brother Sebastian no longer needed to be coddled. He was in a much better place than he'd been in a long time. Heather and her daughter, Ava, had given him his second wind. "He's not answering texts or calls. I don't know what the fuck I'm doing here."

"Have you checked the hospitals?" Sebastian asked. His thoughts naturally went to the worst-case scenario. I understood why, but it didn't fit this situation.

"My guess is that he is somewhere sleeping off a hangover. His father might be right about him not having what it takes to assume any role at their family's company."

"Have you spoken to his father?"

"Since arriving? No. Over the years—plenty. He doesn't think Felix is responsible enough, so he gave him a small project with which he could prove himself without doing any real damage. Felix said he wanted to wow his father . . . bring in a client that would impress him . . . which is why I'm here. I lined up contacts to introduce him to."

"You and Felix used to be tight. I'm sure he'll resurface."

"My feelings aren't hurt, Sebastian. I'm pissed. If I don't hear from him soon, I'll be flying home tonight."

"There's no need to rush back. I have everything under control."

The sun was setting just behind the Musée d'Orsay across the river. Someone else might have been impressed by the sight, but it did nothing for me. For the first time in my life I felt adrift, and it was unsettling.

Sebastian continued, "You always loved Europe. There was a time when we could hardly get you to come back to the States."

Those days felt like another lifetime. Paris had been one of my favorite cities to party in. Back then, my family hadn't been wealthy, but I had been young and unencumbered by responsibility. My plans had been to backpack across Europe for a summer, but a woman, whose name I'd long since forgotten, had invited me to a party. That night I'd met Felix and his friends.

My brothers called me the pretty boy of our family. Broad shoulders. Flat abs. A dick big enough to make even a man look twice in a public shower. None of it was a curse.

Paris had been my playground, and I'd had a sinfully good time in it. Back then, Felix and I had had a lot in common. Women. Parties. Travel. Young and wild, we had felt like there was nothing we couldn't do.

The fun had come to an abrupt stop, though, when Sebastian's first wife died in a car accident. She'd been pregnant, and the loss of both had sent him into a dark place he'd only recently surfaced from. My father had called me home, and I'd gone without hesitation because I knew, had our roles been reversed, Sebastian would have dropped everything for me.

Family first.

The years that followed had been tough for everyone. I'd stepped in when I needed to and stepped back when Sebastian was able to take the lead. Working had been cathartic for my brother, and building financial security for the family had become nearly an obsession for him. Together we'd turned my father's small chain of stores into the multibillion-dollar Romano Superstores. In general, if the job entailed tearing down, threatening, or bulldozing through, Sebastian handled it. If an issue could best be handled with diplomacy, finesse, and charm . . . I took the lead.

I could smooth over almost any situation Sebastian's single-mindedness landed our company in. Since remarrying, Sebastian had become much more levelheaded and no longer required constant damage control. Suddenly he was partnering up with our competition instead of demolishing them.

Romano Superstores was a ship that didn't require two captains. If running the family company was important to me, I could have justified my right to stay at the helm. We'd built it up together. Had I not stepped in each time Sebastian had faltered, we might have lost everything—but I was proud to see my brother standing tall again. I wanted only good things for him.

I just wasn't sure what that meant as far as my role now.

I'd hoped returning to Europe would bring me the answers I'd been seeking. Sadly, all I'd learned was that Felix was still . . . Felix, and I wasn't the playboy I'd once been. I had no desire to hit the clubs or pick up any of the beautiful women I'd exchanged looks with.

So what did I want?

"Gian and Christof are jealous you're in Paris without them." Sebastian's comment pulled my attention back to our conversation. "Gian wants to know why you couldn't have waited until he was on school break."

"I'm sure." I smiled. Both of my younger brothers could afford to travel if they wanted to, but neither had done much of it. For Christof, the comment had likely been a joke. He was a numbers guy. Laid back and steady, like our father. Travel and excitement weren't his thing. Gian, on the other hand, might have actually wanted to come with me. I hadn't asked him, though, because I didn't want him to miss a class. I couldn't have been prouder of him for doing as well as he was at Johns Hopkins in Baltimore.

Attending a college several hours away from home had been a difficult move for him. He'd come to our family because his biological mother, Aunt Rosella, wasn't mentally stable. Technically, he was my cousin, but in my heart he has always been my brother. I swear he's never traveled without us because part of him feared we wouldn't be there when he returned. That was why we'd all gone down to see the school with him—to show him that the distance wouldn't change his place in our family.

It was also why, since then, we'd rotated visiting him with flying him home to Connecticut every other weekend. In my family, a person could wander as far as they wished as long as their ass made it back home for Sunday meals with our parents.

For Gian, the family dinner traveled.

That level of mutual support was why it was impossible to resent Sebastian for wanting full control of the family company again. He hadn't so much as said it, yet it was not only obvious but also a good move for him. He needed the win, and despite how we ribbed each other, at the end of the day my brothers and I were all on the same team. It was time for me to bow out gracefully.

"Mom told me to remind you to see Nonna in Montalcino before you come home. Her pasta alone is worth the trip. Careful, though—the cousins will try to marry you off. They introduced me to every single woman in the town. I kept trying to explain about Heather, but my Italian isn't very good. You're single, though, so who knows? You might come home with a wife who cooks as good as Mom."

I laughed at Sebastian's words. "Tempting as that sounds, I'll skip that trip. Wouldn't want to accidentally end up married."

"You might want to consider settling down. You're not getting any younger."

"Oh my God, you've been married less than a year and you already sound like Dad. Marriage isn't for everyone." Love? My parents, as well as Sebastian and Heather, were living proof that it was real, but I'd never even come close to being in love. I was beginning to doubt I was capable of it. That thought made me a little sad. I loved my family, and it was strange to imagine a future without one of my own—as strange as realizing I didn't know where I belonged now.

I had been given a chance to start over after my brother's return. I had the resources to build something on my own. Was that what I wanted? After so many years of knowing exactly what needed to be done and what role I needed to fill . . . I didn't like how not knowing felt. "I have to go, Sebastian. I'll text you later with my plans."

"You haven't taken a vacation in years, Mauricio. Enjoy Paris."

"Will do."

With that, we ended the phone conversation, and I stepped onto a wooden-floored pedestrian bridge, Pont des Arts: the "love lock" bridge. Plexiglass panels flanked either side in a valiant attempt to stop romantics from around the world from burdening the bridge with a metal symbol of their love. I leaned over the railing and saw a few metal locks tied to a rope near the base of the bridge.

People were idiots. How did anyone consider a lock from a hardware store romantic? Okay, I could see why men would go along with the practice, but . . .

My phone rang again.

Felix. "You're alive," I said with heavy sarcasm.

"Barely." His voice was thick and slurred.

Annoyance swept through me. He sounded stoned. "Where are you?"

"At Pitié-Salpêtrière Hospital. Sorry about our meeting, but I had an emergency surgery."

"Surgery? Are you okay?"

"I'm better than okay. They gave me the best painkillers. I'm feeling good."

"What the hell happened?"

His voice lowered. "Can't tell you, but I need you to do me a favor."

I glanced to my right and realized a backpacker was actively listening to my conversation. I walked away as I said, "Whatever you need, but what do you mean you can't tell me?"

His voice was a loud whisper. "It's better if you don't know."

I'd probably watched too much *CSI*, but I instantly imagined him with a bullet wound. What had Felix gotten into this time? As a rule, I stayed on the right side of the law, but for a friend in need, I'd do what had to be done.

Unless he'd done something so fucking stupid that he deserved the consequence.

"I'm not doing shit unless you're up-front with me, Felix."

He made a pained sound, and I felt like an ass. For all I knew he'd just received a terminal diagnosis and was fighting to sound brave.

Felix? Brave?

"I broke my dick," he mumbled.

"You what?"

"It's called a penile fracture."

"How the fuck did you break your dick?" As I said the words, maybe a little too loud, I glanced around. An older couple shot each other a look. The man, in his eighties if he was a day old, cringed as his wife graciously looked away.

"How do you think? Remember I said I was working in my father's office now? Well, a friend came to visit me. I thought I could squeeze a little fun in before my first meeting of the day. I was rushing—"

I lowered my voice. "Okay, too much information. What do you need me to do?"

"Remember I told you about Cecile?"

"The Englishwoman? I didn't know you were still seeing her."

"It's on and off. When she has time off, she comes to see me. Nothing serious. But she's staying at my apartment right now."

"I'm surprised she didn't go to the hospital with you."

"She wasn't the friend I fucked at the office."

"Ah. Gotcha."

"And she can't know about this. Any of this. I can't be the man with the broken dick."

In the scheme of things, that didn't seem like the most important aspect of this, but no man would want that label. "How broken is it?"

"Bad enough that I had surgery, but if I take a month off from sex, I should be fine. The doctor said he has seen much worse. Sometimes they blow up like eggplants."

"Stop. I got it." I did not want to picture that. Ever. And now it was all I could.

"I knew something bad had happened when I heard the pop. It didn't hurt as much as the doctor said it could have, but it was like a little deflated purple balloon."

"Oh my God. I'll do whatever you want if you promise to stop talking about this."

"I'm just saying it could have been worse."

"I'm glad it wasn't. Now what about Cecile?"

"I'm being discharged tomorrow, and I'd like to hide out at my place. You need to get her out of my apartment. Tell her I had to leave town on business. Tell her I've been arrested. I don't give a shit. Just don't tell her where I am or what happened, and make sure she gets home safely."

From the stories Felix had shared over the years about Cecile, that might not be easy. She owned a mirror-manufacturing company that she'd started on her own. She was a self-made millionaire and proud of it. Intelligent. Beautiful. What she saw in Felix had always been a mystery to me, but some women enjoyed the challenge of trying to change a man.

If she found out Felix had been with another woman during her time with him, he might end up more broken than he already was. Lie to her? Try to escort her home? Neither were things I could imagine going well.

I wasn't even a good liar. I'd much rather slap the truth down and let people do with it what they will.

I've never broken my dick, though.

I'd like to think Felix was a good enough friend to cover for me if our situations were reversed. "Okay. Send me her number and I'll see what I can do."

"You might have to go to my apartment. She's anti–cell phone when she's in Paris. She says it's the only way she can unwind."

I flexed my neck to one side. This was getting better and better. *Fuck.* "Is she there now?"

"Probably. She said she was bringing a friend from college over for dinner. Some American woman. I don't remember her name. *Dinner* is our code word for a threesome. Shit, I can't think about that right now. I'm not allowed to get excited."

I rubbed a hand over my forehead. Felix hadn't changed at all. "I'll do what I can, but this sounds like a real clusterfuck. If I go to your apartment and Cecile's not there, I'm not camping out until she comes back. I'll check you into a room somewhere else, and you can figure this shit out on your own when you're clearheaded."

He sighed. "She'll be there. I wonder if her friend is hot."

"You have problems. You know that, right?"

Felix laughed, a clear sign that he was still flying high. "I know. Don't tell anyone what happened, okay? Especially not my family. I told my father I did this by walking into a doorknob. It was the best story I could come up with at the time."

"God, Felix."

"God is right. I've been praying like a bastard since it happened."

It was my turn to laugh. "I'll text you later."

I ended the call and realized the older couple was still watching me. The older woman raised her square tinted glasses and smiled at me. "We hope your friend recovers quickly."

"Ice," her husband said with a straight face. "A lot of ice."

I nodded and walked away. There wasn't a question I could ask him that I wanted to know the answer to.

CHAPTER THREE

WREN

"Just do it. What are you afraid of?"

Afraid wasn't how I'd describe what I felt when my friend Cecile whipped her bikini top off and tossed it on the floor beside the partially concealed terrace hot tub we were sitting in. *Uncomfortable. Awkward. Embarrassed.* I looked away and kept my top on. "Nudity has never been my thing."

"Maybe it's time you try it." Her tone was amused, but not cruel. Nothing about my current behavior should surprise her. We'd attended the same college in New York. I didn't skinny-dip with her back then; that much hadn't changed about me. "There is nothing shameful about the human form."

"I agree." I did. In theory. I just couldn't help that I'd been raised with closed doors by fully dressed parents. Once . . . once I'd walked in on my mother changing, and she'd locked her bedroom door ever since. I'd had a great childhood. Wonderful parents. We just didn't do naked. Ever.

"Tell me you've had sex."

I turned to glare at her. "You know I have. There was golfer boy freshman year. Then creepy guy from the third floor senior year. Remember how he followed me around for months afterward?"

"I mean recently."

My cheeks warmed. "Of course I have."

"When?"

I counted on my fingers. Then sighed. In months, I'd need more than my fingers and toes. In years . . . it was depressing to think in those terms. "It's been a while."

She rolled her eyes and tucked a curl back into her loose bun. "I'm glad you came to Paris. I worry about you."

I tried not to get defensive, but I couldn't help it. "Because I didn't become a millionaire like you?"

Luckily, Cecile knew me too well to take offense. Even though we hadn't seen each other in years, we'd stayed in touch. She was like family to me. The good kind of family, the ones you want to see at the holidays. "You could have if that had been your goal. I admire that you chose to move home and help support your family. It's just . . ."

"Just what?"

"I remember why you went into engineering, and it wasn't to pay your parents' mortgage. How is your father?"

With close friends there were no secrets. No shame. "Same. He still has good days and bad days."

"I'm sorry."

"Don't be. He does the best he can. Isn't that all any of us can do?"

"I guess. Is he still too stubborn to wear a prosthetic arm?"

I sighed. "Stubborn. Proud. He says none of them do what he needs them to. I used to think I—" I stopped there. There'd been a time when my interest in engineering had been about sharing a common passion with him. My father was brilliant. If his life had taken a different route, he might have done something history would remember him for. When I was younger, I believed I was born to create something with him—for him. Like a child dreaming of becoming a famous singer or a superhero. Eventually reality stepped in, and I chose more realistic goals. Now, when I left him smiling, I let that be my achievement. "He has yet to find one he likes."

"Are you happy, Wren? I'm only asking because I care. Is something wrong?"

I closed my eyes and leaned back against the neck cushion. Was I happy? I hadn't allowed myself the luxury of that selfish question.

What was happiness?

I had a good life. I was healthy. I had friends. Enough money to be able to help my parents. What did I have to complain about?

But happy? I didn't know if I would have gone as far as to say that. Most days I focused on the positive in my life, because I refused to add the weight of my discontent onto either of my parents. Being so far away from them allowed me the freedom to be honest. "I hate my job." The admission burst out of me. I opened my eyes and looked across at Cecile.

Although we talked regularly, I hadn't laid this topic at her door. Her success with her manufacturing company was incredible. I celebrated her success rather than face my own situation. There was no benefit to lamenting what wasn't. Still, it felt good to vent for once. "It's so fucking boring. All I do is visually inspect sprinkler systems. I walk around with a tablet, taking notes. That's what I do with my mechanical engineering degree. And if something is broken, I'm not even the one who fixes it."

"Then why do it?" Easy for a millionaire who had been raised by two healthy, upper-middle-class parents to say. Still, it was a question worth addressing.

How had I painted myself into this corner? "It's stable money. Good benefits. You know I wanted something near to my parents, and NE FireSP offered me a job right out of college."

"You chose safe over fulfilling." She reached behind her, filled a glass with champagne, and handed it to me.

Yep, that sounds about right. I downed half of it. "I did what I had to do." My defense sounded hollow to even my own ears.

She reached for a glass of her own. "Did you? I get the path you chose. I get *you*. All I'm suggesting is that it might be time to reevaluate that life plan."

"I can't. My mother isn't able to work as much as she once could. Some of their bills have become my bills." I raised my hand in a plea. "Before you say anything—I *want* to help them. My parents are everything to me."

Cecile filled a flute of champagne for herself. "I don't doubt that. You're a good person, Wren, but you can't put aside your life for theirs. What are you afraid of? What do you think would happen if you did something for yourself?"

Her question tapped at a fear I usually denied. My father was a good man, but I'd grown up in the shadow of his demons. I knew exactly what I feared would happen if he lost his battle with them. Just thinking about it had me downing the rest of my glass in one gulp. "Nothing I could live with. My mom can't handle my father on her own," I said with a shrug of resignation. "They need me." It was that simple and that complicated. No, it wasn't fair that I wasn't as free as many people my age were—but life wasn't fair. If it were, my father would have come home from his time in the army holding his head high like the hero he was, and not as a broken man none of us had ever found a way to heal. I let Cecile refill my glass. "I'm sorry. I don't mean to be such a downer."

Compassion and love met my gaze. "Hey, don't be sorry. I love you. I just wish I knew what to say. I don't know what it's like to have someone rely on me the way your parents rely on you. If there's anything I can do . . ."

I gave her hand a squeeze. "You already have. You invited me to Paris. You don't know how much I needed this vacation—to step out of my life for just a little while. This is the perfect way to recharge my batteries. I'm not unhappy, Cecile. Everyone has responsibilities. I don't resent mine; I just always thought I'd be more than I am . . ."

Her hand tightened on mine. "Stop right there. Don't you dare say a bad word about my best friend. You are—"

"Enough about me," I said, needing to end the conversation that was making me think about things I'd wanted to forget for a week. I forced a smile and dropped her hand. "How long have you had this place?"

"Did I say I own it?" Her head cocked to the side.

"Are you renting?" I took another look around. Glass and chrome with mahogany accents. Expensive, but with a masculine feel to it that upon consideration didn't match Cecile's style. Not nearly enough mirrors.

"No. Do you remember I told you about Felix?"

"Once-a-month Felix? You're still seeing him? I thought you said that was over."

She took a long sip of champagne, then raised both arms to place them on the edge of the hot tub, bringing her breasts fully above the bubbles. I must have been buzzed by then, because it no longer felt awkward. "I did end it, but other men drive me crazy. They're so needy. Felix is just easy. It's like visiting a fuck spa."

"A *fuck spa*," I repeated with a laugh. Yeah, I was buzzed.

"You have no idea how good sex is when there is no pressure to make it into something meaningful. I don't ask Felix who he's with when I'm not here. He doesn't ask me. If I skip a month, I don't have to explain why. It's just sex. Really good sex."

With round eyes, I looked away again. "Sounds . . ."

"Therapeutic," she finished for me. "I swear, there's no better way to relax. You should try it."

A flush warmed my cheeks again. "That's not my thing either."

She laughed. "Sex?"

"Sex outside of a relationship."

"Oh. And how long has it been since you've been in a relationship?"

I cringed. Part of what I've always loved about Cecile was that she didn't filter her opinions. Her description of sex with Felix could easily have fit our friendship. No pressure. No stress. We called each other when the mood struck us and didn't sweat the times we didn't call. There were two sides of Cecile, the savvy businesswoman and the free spirit she chose to be in her downtime.

We were very different, but somehow it worked. The key was appreciating those differences and occasionally giving each other shit for them—but all in fun. With Cecile I'd never had to be anyone but myself, and when you find a friend like that . . . you keep them for life. "Two years," I admitted.

"Oh Lord, you need to get laid. Don't be offended, but I'm going to throw an offer out there. Felix will be back soon. If you want to stay, you're welcome to."

My eyes snapped to hers, and I swallowed hard. "Stay?"

"For dinner."

Relief flooded through me, and I chuckled. "I'm sorry. For a second I thought—"

"That I was suggesting a ménage à trois?"

"Yes."

"I was. Felix and I like to spice things up every once in a while. No pressure. But think about it."

As a knee-jerk reaction, I stood up and stuttered, "I—I—I love you for asking. It's a huge compliment. Huge. When you asked me if I wanted to come see you in Paris, I didn't think you meant *see* you." I waved my hand at her bare chest. I did love her, and we were close, but I didn't want more than that.

Nor did I want to offend her.

"Wren?"

"Yes?" I put a leg over the edge of the hot tub. Buzzed or not, it was time to get out.

"You realize you could simply say no."

I really should have used the steps to get out. The drop was higher on that side than I'd thought. I was dangling over the side of the hot tub. Cecile's tone was so calm, so nonjudgmental, I felt ridiculous for bolting. Still, I needed to be clear. "No."

In true Cecile style, her smile remained effortless and genuine. "That's settled then. Now, would you like some help? I'd hate for you to break a leg on your first day in Paris." She stood and held out her hand.

I took it. There was a twinkle in her eye that made me wonder if she'd suggested a threesome just to shock me out of the funk I'd fallen into.

She hauled me back over the rim of the hot tub. I hit the water with a splash that had us both laughing.

"I did knock," a deep male voice announced, and I froze.

Even though I still had my bathing suit on, I ducked into the water. When I turned toward the entrance to the balcony, my breath caught in my throat. I was still a no go on a threesome, but if I ever did have one, it would be because of someone like him.

A little green monster nipped at my heels. I wasn't envious by nature. Some people had more than I did. Some people had less. But Cecile had *him*.

I totally understand her fuck spa now.

I'd lost my voice, but not my sight. I started at the tip of his leather dress shoes, let my gaze wander up his legs. He filled out his trousers in a way few men do . . . and the rest of him was deliciously muscular and . . . oh my God, was he getting a hard-on?

I forced my eyes higher and reminded myself that he was Cecile's. *Sure, they have an open relationship and she pretty much already asked me to have sex with him, but . . .* I gulped . . . *girl code, right? I shouldn't be this attracted to someone who essentially belongs to one of my friends.*

What am I saying? People don't belong to people.

This guy is scrambling my brain.

I looked him over again. I could have stopped at his wide shoulders, but I had to know if his face was as . . . Oh yeah. Square jaw. Dark stubble growing in. Eyes so brown they were almost black.

When our eyes met, a crazy warmth spread through me. I started playing Never Have I Ever with myself. Never have I ever thought a man's mouth looked so kissable. Never have I ever wanted to lose my inhibitions and do something spontaneous I was sure to regret.

How much do women touch each other during threesomes? Could I ask for none at all? I frowned as I imagined that scenario. No, I wouldn't want to share him.

I shook my head in wonder.

This is lust.

Or too much champagne.

I ducked deeper beneath the water.

Probably the champagne. I need to get out of here.

CHAPTER FOUR
MAURICIO

Another man might have thought he'd hit a sexual lottery by walking in on what I had, but one of these women, the topless brunette if I remembered Felix's description correctly, was off my list of possible hookups, simply because it was never good to mix friends and fucks. You can fuck your friends; you just can't fuck your friends' fucks. It was a rule that had served me well over the years.

Now the blonde—I'd gotten only a glimpse of her, but one glimpse had been enough to convince my cock she was not on the do-not-touch list. I wasn't looking for a threesome, but if she was interested, I wouldn't mind giving double the effort to her pleasure.

If she doesn't drown herself.

Even while giving me a bold once-over, she'd dipped lower and lower beneath the water until all that was visible above the side of the hot tub was the top of her head and her eyes—wide, big, and difficult to look away from.

"You must be Mauricio," the brunette said, and I reluctantly turned my attention back to her. She calmly stepped out of the hot tub and retrieved her top. As casual as if she were donning a jacket over an outfit, she put it back on. Nudity was nothing new to me. In fact, the natural-ness of it was what I'd always liked about Europe. The female body, in all its beautiful shapes and sizes, was a work of art. Why should it be hidden away? "I'm Cecile. I recognize you from old photos of you and Felix together. You've aged well."

"Thank you. Felix's taste in women has improved, I see." She was a beautiful woman in her late twenties—tight body, comfortable with her own sexuality. In other circumstances I might have found that attractive, but my attention kept returning to the mostly submerged woman in the hot tub.

"You're quite the charmer," Cecile said, but not flirtatiously, and I was grateful for that. My goal was to convince her to leave.

I dipped my head in recognition of the compliment. "Felix asked me to drop by with a message. I'll give you ladies time to dry off, and then we can talk in the living room."

My gaze met the blonde's again, and I couldn't help the grin that spread across my face. Her shyness didn't appear to be an act. I couldn't imagine her engaging in a wild romp with Felix and Cecile.

I *could* imagine joining her in the hot tub, though, and kissing every inch of her that I convinced to rise above the water. How bold would she become when I asked her to tell me what she liked?

My cock was at full mast and aching from the images I was torturing myself with. I turned on my heel and strode back into the penthouse. *Down, boy.*

I walked behind the bar area and poured myself a glass of water. The shelves were well stocked, with only the best of every liquor, but I needed to keep my wits about me. Cecile was no pushover. Getting her to leave without much explanation wasn't going to be easy.

She donned a terry-cloth wrap and came to sit at the bar. I poured her a glass of water and placed it in front of her. Her eyebrows rose and fell, but she sipped at the drink. "So what did Felix ask you to tell me?"

I cleared my throat. "He was called away on business—"

Her laughter interrupted my excuse, and she raised a hand for me to stop. "Felix? He'll be lucky if his father trusts him with filing. Don't waste my time with lies."

Okay. "That's all I have." The lie. I'd already promised I wouldn't tell her the truth. "It was just as much of a surprise to me. I flew over for a business meeting with him. He did ask me, though, to make sure you got home okay."

Her head cocked to the side, and she tapped her fingers on the surface of the bar. "He knows I have my own plane. This rings weird to me. What are you not telling me?"

"I've said all I can." That much was true.

Dressed in jeans and a blouse, but deliciously barefoot, the blonde joined us, and I forgot what we were talking about. *Broken what? Who cares.*

Her hair was damp on the ends but hung loose past her shoulders. She wasn't thin, but the way she filled out those jeans was sinful. I've always liked an ass I could grab, and she was rounded in all the right places. Although they were chastely covered, her tits were my favorite size . . . big enough to bury my face between. She took a seat next to Cecile and looked me right in the eye.

All too vividly I imagined looking down into those blue eyes of hers while she was wrapped around my waist and we fucked until neither of us could move. *I might want to stay in Paris after all.*

Cecile broke into my fantasy with, "Wren, this is Felix's friend, Mauricio."

"It's a pleasure to meet you." I held out my hand for a shake. I could have gone in for the French double-kiss greeting, but enough of my blood had already headed south. I needed to calm down. I couldn't remember the last time a woman had gotten me that excited without even trying. I let go of her hand and gave her my signature smile—the one more than one woman had claimed had closed the deal with them.

"Nice to meet you too," she said and blushed as if not used to sustained attention from a man. Her American accent was familiar—East Coast, New England. Funny how small the world was.

Not looking pleased with the idea, Cecile said, "Mauricio was just explaining to me that Felix left town." To me she added, "Attractive as you are, I hope Felix didn't send you over in his place."

Wren's mouth rounded in surprise. I poured a glass of water for her as well. I'd never needed the advantage of alcohol, and I could already tell she was attracted to me. After that, it was simply a matter of time, and there was no way I was flying back to the States before having her. We had next-level sexual attraction—no man with a working dick walked away from that.

"For *dinner*, you mean?" I asked in a purr, only because I wanted to see Wren's reaction to the possibility.

Her eyes widened, and in a breathy voice she said, "I—I—I already explained that I prefer to eat alone." Her hand flew to her mouth, and in a rush she added, "Not alone. I eat with people, just not at crowded tables." She groaned and took a long sip of her water.

I looked back and forth between the two women and wondered at their relationship. They seemed comfortable with each other, but not in the way Felix had implied. "Good. I'm not here for the food, at least not anything from my friend's kitchen."

With a wave of her hand, Cecile said, "Okay, before you give my friend a heart attack, I'm calling a halt to this."

My attention remained on Wren. I leaned a little closer, lowered my voice, and asked, "Sorry, am I coming on too strong? So I shouldn't ask you to leave with me? Have a meal. Just the two of us?"

While gulping down more water, Wren began to choke. Her face went deep red. She stood and gasped for breath between coughs. I walked around to her side of the bar. Concern momentarily replaced desire. "Are you okay?"

I gave her back a pat, and she belched. If she'd been embarrassed before, she looked ten times that when she realized how loud it had been. It was adorable.

"Oh my God. It's the bubbles from the champagne," she croaked. "I don't usually drink at all."

"Those bubbles will get you every time." I laughed. "Okay now?"

The deep breaths she took brushed the side of one of her breasts against my arm, and heat rushed through me. I stepped back because it was already too tempting to kiss her despite our disapproving chaperone. Alone with Wren, that bar would have been the perfect height for how I was imagining starting my exploration of her.

Her tongue flicked across her bottom lip. Oh yes, we were on the same page. Time to lose Cecile. I cleared my throat. "So, work will keep Felix off the grid for a while. He said he'd call you when he's feeling—when he's back in town."

In the throbbing silence that followed, Cecile sighed. "I don't believe you about where Felix is, but if he doesn't want me to know what he's up to, I'm reasonably certain I don't care to hear the details. You can tell him I'll be out of here in the morning, and he is welcome to call me, or not, when he returns." She stood and walked over to the door of the apartment. "Thank you for delivering his message."

Wren opened her mouth, then shut it as if changing her mind. "Nice to meet you, Mauricio."

I wasn't one to give up that easily. I looked around, found a pen, and wrote my number on a paper napkin. As I handed it to her, I purred into her ear, "I'm in Paris for several more days. Call me."

I heard the catch in her breath and saw desire flame in her eyes. I didn't need to pursue. She'd call.

I told myself to step back and walk out of there with a clear victory. I remained rooted, though, looking down at her until I gave in to the pull and brushed my lips over hers. Softly. Just a taste.

Her mouth opened slightly, and my tongue swept in. Hers danced with mine briefly. Hot honey and fire. I was barely in control when I lifted my head and stepped back.

She raised a hand to her lips. I waited. Would she leave with me? She wanted to. "Goodbye, Mauricio," she said in a husky voice.

It was a struggle not to kiss her again. "Talk to you tomorrow," I said, then winked.

Cecile opened the door as I approached it. She was shaking her head with disapproval. As I passed by her, she placed a hand on my chest to halt me. "I'll get my own place, but I'm not leaving Paris. I invited Wren for a visit, and her safety is my responsibility."

I frowned. "I've never hurt a woman in my life."

She lowered her voice so only I could hear. "I know your history, Mauricio. Stay away from my friend. You're not her type."

"Shouldn't that be her choice?" I couldn't help but add, "Or are you jealous because I'm the one she won't turn down?"

She dropped her hand, and a smooth, cold smile stretched her lips. "There are very few people I give a shit about, but Wren is one of them. Break her heart and I'll kill you."

"Her heart? I'm not looking for anything that intense."

"I know." With that, Cecile closed the door in my face.

CHAPTER FIVE

WREN

No matter how far I was from home, what I'd just realized was that I was still painfully, awkwardly, myself. I don't know what other women do when they encounter drop-dead gorgeous men who show interest in them. I hid, said almost nothing, nearly choked to death, belched, kissed him like I knew him, then said goodbye as if everything that had happened was normal.

I looked down at the napkin in my hand. "Talk to you tomorrow," he'd said with a wink. Cocky bastard. Oh yes, because whatever I'd come to Paris for, he was certain he could deliver.

Physically impressive? Yes.

Humble? No.

But that kiss . . . it had lit something in me, a yearning so strong that not kissing him back hadn't been a possibility.

Cecile came to stand beside me. "Don't even think about it." She reached for the napkin, but I stuffed it in my jeans pocket.

"I'm not going to call him." Even as I made the affirmation, I wasn't sure I meant it.

Hand on hip, she challenged, "Listen, I'm the last one to judge anyone's decisions. You do what you want, but that guy—he's a player. You'll only get hurt."

Okay, hang on. "Didn't you just tell me I needed to loosen up? You have a *fuck spa*. One you invited me to *dinner* at. How would seeing this guy be worse?" I made a pained face. "Not that being with you and Felix would have been bad, just crowded." I stopped there because it was uncharted territory to me and I didn't want to offend her.

She threw up her hands. "You don't need to justify your refusal. It was just an offer I tossed out. Let's move past it." She walked behind the bar and poured herself a glass of rosé. "Want one?"

I shook my head. "I caught a buzz from the champagne." I groaned. "I can't believe I burped in front of Mauricio. It's really not hard to figure out why it's been so long since I've had sex."

Wineglass in hand, Cecile sat down on the white leather couch. "Stop. You're beautiful. All you need is a little confidence. Men are not complicated. Feed them. Fuck them. Let them have their freedom. Really, that's it."

I sat beside her, tucking my feet beneath me. Despite loving her as I did, I wasn't sure Cecile was my best choice as a relationship guru. "I'd like to think there's more to them than that."

Cecile laughed. "Maybe it's me, but I prefer to keep things simple. I like my men the same way. Mauricio fits the description of my type, and that's how I know he's wrong for you. If Felix had come back and you had stayed, that would have just been about having fun. Tomorrow, maybe things would have felt a little awkward at first, but we'd be solid. Sex. No sex. We'd still be friends. Mauricio's the kind of guy who sweeps you off your feet for a week, feeds you a whole fantasy, then doesn't know your name the next time you meet up. Look me in the eye and tell me you could handle that."

My shoulders slumped. "I don't know. I've never been swept off my feet. I've had sex. No sweeping. Nothing worth bragging about."

Cecile took another sip of wine and pursed her lips before she said, "I do think you need to get laid. And you could do a lot worse than that guy. Maybe I'm wrong. I'd just hate to see you get hurt."

When your wild friend cautioned you not to do something, it was hard to dismiss her concerns. Objectively speaking, I didn't know a single thing about Mauricio. Couldn't even claim we had exchanged witty dialogue that won me over. Anything I might have with him would be purely on a superficial level. "You're right. Sleeping with him would be wrong."

"Hold on. I didn't say that. As long as it happens between two consenting adults, it's not my definition of wrong. It's about knowing yourself, sweetie, and being true to that." She finished her glass of wine and placed it on the coffee table. "Stop looking at me like I'm going to pounce on you. I forgot how sexually uptight you are."

"I'm not uptight." It wasn't her offer that had me wound up. Meeting Mauricio had left me nervous, excited, my stomach fluttering in a good way. The freedom of having a friend like Cecile was that I could be myself. No pretense. No guilt. I sat forward with a smile. "Honestly, I was a little jealous when I thought Mauricio was Felix. I work in a man's field. I'm surrounded by men all day long. I don't usually get all tongue-tied and goofy. I hear what you're saying about Mauricio being a player. If I were home and he was working across the hall from me, I wouldn't even consider calling him. But . . . a part of me thinks . . . what happens in Paris stays in Paris, right?"

Cecile hooted with laughter. "Look at you—this guy really revved your engines, didn't he?"

My smile was huge and unapologetic. "He did."

She gave me a long look. "If Felix were here, I'd ask him more about Mauricio. I know they've been friends for a long time. They ran wild together all over Europe for a few years. Felix has a lot of respect for him. Does that make him a safe Paris fling for you? I don't know. Definitely use condoms."

My jaw dropped, and I threw a pillow at her. "I'm a little old for the sex talk, don't you think?"

"I saw you with him. When an attraction is that strong, even someone as practical as you might get impulsive and slip up. Remember, if you're not comfortable enough with a man to ask him to put on a raincoat, you have no business fucking him."

Female wisdom by Cecile. I could make a T-shirt empire based solely on her one-liners.

I took the napkin out of my pocket and looked at it. "I might call him, but that doesn't mean I'm going to sleep with him. Do you know how many dates I've been on that have gone nowhere?" I didn't remember how a single one of those men kissed, but there'd been a heat to Mauricio's kiss I wouldn't soon forget.

A heat I wanted to experience again.

Cecile stood. "I'm going to change out of this wet bathing suit. What do you want to do tonight?"

I was exhausted from the flight over, but also excited to be in a city I'd always dreamed of visiting. "I don't have the energy for a club, but would you be up for a walk? The room I rented is on Rue Washington."

"Right off the Champs-Élysées. Touristy, but there are nice hotels in the area. Sure, let's walk around, and I'll choose a place near where you're staying. What do you have?"

"A one bedroom I found online."

She nodded. Being with Cecile again reminded me of why we'd remained friends for as long as we had. I didn't need to check into the Four Seasons to impress her, and she didn't need to explain why she wanted to. Some people thought their friends had to be identical to them—in politics, religions, world views. I disagreed. What a boring world it would be if we were all the same. "Do you think you'll be moved over early? Tomorrow I thought I'd start with a . . ."

"Don't say hop-on hop-off bus."

I stuck out my tongue at her. "You are here all the time, Cecile. I've never been. I want to do touristy things. Come on. How bad could it be?"

"Wren, I will walk your ass all over this town if you want me to, but there is no way in hell I'm riding a bus with you."

I waved the napkin at her. "Oh, really? Well, then, I'll just ask someone else."

Smiling, she shook her head. "You think he'd go with you? He might agree to meet you, but tour the city in a bus with headphones, snapping photos with you? Not his scene."

I stood and posed, putting my hands first on my hips, then in my hair. "You're underestimating my charm." Then I snorted.

And she laughed. "I just might be." Her expression sobered. "You do need to be careful, but now you've piqued my curiosity. He was interested, but enough for a hop-on hop-off bus? That's a good test of how far he's willing to go to fuck you."

"I don't test my dates." I rolled my eyes. "And is everything about sex with you?"

Her grin was the same back in college, and I loved it. "In Paris it is."

Also smiling, I waved toward the hallway that led to the bedrooms. "Go change. I want to find some tacky souvenirs to take back to my coworkers. Like an Eiffel Tower keychain. Or those pens where the person is dressed until you tip the pen and then they're naked. Do you know where they sell those?"

"This is going to be a long week," Cecile joked as she headed down the hall.

Once alone, I smoothed out the napkin and traced the numbers written on it. I could tour Paris on my own. I didn't need to call him. In fact, it might be better if I didn't. If I went back home without seeing him again, he would be a harmless, flirty memory I had from my first night in Paris.

If I asked him to spend the day playing tourist with me and he wasn't interested, it would be a disappointing start to the first vacation I'd taken in years.

On the other hand, if he said yes . . .

Cecile had called me practical, and that was essentially how I saw myself. I didn't make rash decisions. When given two paths, I chose the more responsible one.

But I was on vacation—in *Paris*.

The city of love.

Twenty-seven years of making good choices, of being the person others could rely on . . . hadn't I earned a little vacation from that as well? That was all this would be.

Cecile was back, dressed in flats, a loose off-white sweater, and dark slacks. Simple yet eye-catching.

"Ready?" she asked.

I stuffed Mauricio's phone number in the front pocket of my jeans. "Let's go."

A short time later, arm in arm, Cecile and I were strolling down the busy Champs-Élysées. We window-shopped at stores I didn't need to go into to know I couldn't afford anything from. That didn't take away from my euphoria. Traffic flew by us. The sidewalks were packed with other people who were clearly as new to the city as I was. There was an energy in the air that was electric.

Not to mention how giddy it made me that everywhere I looked there was another architectural marvel. The Arc de Triomphe was stunning architecturally. People disappeared down and emerged from the Métro steps. They were from all over the world, and I would have liked to hear the stories of what had brought each of them to Paris.

The street was lit, as were the canopies of several restaurants. An expensive car pulled over and someone emerged, but almost no one stopped to see who. The crowd was more engrossed in a male street performer playing a guitar and singing a ballad with a voice that belonged on the radio.

I paused, tugging on Cecile's arm. "Do you believe in love at first sight? Because I am in love with this city already."

She paused. At first I thought she was taking a moment to appreciate the lighting along the street, but then I sensed a sadness, a weariness I didn't associate with my larger-than-life friend. "I've missed seeing the world through your eyes, Wren. No, I don't believe in love at first sight. I don't put much stock in the idea of love at all. Perhaps that's why Felix is perfect for me."

I stopped and searched her face. "Or why he's not. Don't settle for safe, Cecile. You are too amazing to be with someone who doesn't see that. Don't let him dismiss you like he did."

Her chin rose. "Like I have much of a choice. In my place, what would you have done?"

I took a moment to consider my response. "Me? I would have called his parents to see if he was okay. Do you know them?"

Her eyes widened. "His parents? No. We've never met." She frowned. "Besides, he can't be unwell. He hasn't been sick a day since I met him. The man has a killer immune system. More likely he's with another woman."

I tossed her earlier words back at her. "Listen, I'm the last one to judge anyone's decisions. You do what you want, but that Felix—he's a player. You want to scare him? Have lunch with his parents." A thought occurred to me. "But never dinner. That would be taking things too far."

"Indeed it would." Her laugh rang out. "Call his parents? How absolutely devious. And here I thought you were the nicer one of us."

"Oh, I'm nice. But I'm no pushover. I don't like the way he sent his friend over to get rid of you."

We began to walk again. She mused aloud, "I don't like that either." We stopped at a crosswalk, and she turned to me. "I'll make you a deal. Text me tomorrow morning after you talk to Mauricio. If he agrees to your early-morning Paris tour and actually gets his ass on that bus, I'll contact Felix's parents."

"You're on."

CHAPTER SIX

WREN

After getting up early and dressing in simple black jeans and a teal T-shirt, I paced the area beside my bed. "Hello, Mauricio, want to come out to play?" I shot for a seductive tone as I asked the empty room. No. I cleared my throat and tried again. "Oh, is this Mauricio? I must have butt dialed you."

I picked up my phone and hunted around for the napkin on the bedside table. I swore when I saw it had gotten wet from the water bottle I'd placed beside it. Shit.

I spread it out. Two of the numbers were smudged, the last one to the point of no longer being legible. It could have been a five. Or an eight. Possibly a six. Double shit.

With the napkin in one hand and my phone in the other, I dialed the numbers I could read and guessed that the last was a five.

If I'm meant to see him, this will be his number.

It rang once.

It rang twice.

A teenage boy's voice came on and said, "You've reached Todd. If you're not a loser, leave a message."

I ended the call.

Okay, it was not a five.

I tried with an eight.

It rang once.

It rang twice.

If this works, I am meant to meet him.

"Hello? Who is this?" a woman demanded.

Oh, crap, I hope he's not married. "I'm looking for Mauricio . . ." I would have provided his last name had I known it. Realizing how little I actually knew about him took a little wind out of my sails.

"You have the wrong number," the woman said and abruptly ended the call.

Frowning down at the napkin, I decided the smudged numeral had to be a six.

Had to.

If it's not a six, I'm done.

We're done.

He probably wouldn't have lived up to his own hype anyway.

I tried the number with a six and held my breath.

It rang once.

It rang twice.

"Speak," a deep male voice commanded.

The memory of his kiss was so vivid I ran my tongue across my bottom lip and relived it. If things worked out, that memory would soon be a reality.

"Hello?" he asked with less patience. "Is someone there?"

I hesitated. Forgot how to speak. Before I had a chance to regain my composure, he hung up. "No," I exclaimed. "No. No. No." I shook my phone in frustration.

Okay. Breathe.

I pressed the number again before I lost the courage to. As soon as he answered, I said, "Hi. It's Wren."

"Wren." I loved the way his voice deepened when he said my name. "Did Cecile give you permission to call me?"

It was a taunt, but a playful one. "She did. We actually have a bet going about what the outcome of this call will be."

"You do? Now that sounds like something we should discuss in person."

Deep breath. "How about now?"

He chuckled. "I'm still in bed, but that's not a problem for me if it's not for you."

Imagining how he might look—bare chested, with just a white sheet draped across his lower half—made me almost forget what I'd planned to do that morning. I shook my head. "Actually, I am heading outside. I've never been to Paris, and I'd like to see the city."

"At eight o'clock in the morning?" His tone implied he couldn't imagine what might be out there to see at that time.

My heart sank a little. Cecile was probably right. Someone like him wouldn't be interested in playing tourist. He'd been clear about what he wanted. I ran my thumb over my lips. I wanted that, too, but I'd heard Cecile's warning. Mauricio would sell me a fantasy, then forget my name.

His fantasy.

Not mine.

Whatever happened between us, if anything at all happened, I refused to be that easy to forget. If he wanted a chance with me, he would have to step into my fantasy . . . how I'd always imagined visiting Paris would be—and part of that included getting up early to ooh and aah over landmarks.

If he said no? Well, then I'd saved myself from the experience of having him one day send a friend to tell me to leave his apartment. Birds of a feather, isn't that what they said? Cecile still hadn't heard from Felix. I didn't want to mean that little to a man . . . not even for a weeklong fling.

I cleared my throat. "Yes. I'm already up and dressed. There's a bus tour, the kind that lets you hop on and hop off at all the tourist sights. That's my plan for the day. Would you like to join me?"

"You're serious?"

"I am." I cringed. I've never been good at flirting. It was the engineer in me. I'd always been straightforward. No games.

He made a sound deep in his throat like a man who was rolling over in bed. "I'd love to spend today with you, but with one condition."

"And what would that be?" My throat went dry. If he said dinner, I was hanging up.

"You allow me to plan how we spend tomorrow."

My heart raced. Mauricio had starred in a delightfully dirty dream the night before, the details of which were vividly replaying in my mind, making it difficult to speak. This was what two years of celibacy did to a person—I couldn't even remember if I'd answered him.

I took a deep breath. It was only fair to warn him. "I am not wild by nature. In fact, I might be considered the opposite of wild. Like boring. If you're looking for—"

"Why don't you let me worry about what I'm looking for. Where do you want to meet?"

I gave him the address where I'd read we could buy tickets for the bus. "Could you be there in an hour?"

"I'm not that far from there, so with a shower and a brisk walk, yes. See you at nine."

"Nine," I repeated and pressed the icon to end the call.

Mauricio had said yes.

I called Cecile. "Hold on to your panties, my friend. Mauricio said yes."

Cecile groaned. "What time is it?"

I checked the digital clock near the bed. "Eight fifteen."

She yawned. "Most people sleep in on vacations."

"Not when they're in Paris and want to beat the rush. Are you still at Felix's place?"

"Yes. I scheduled check-in at the Seasons for around noon." She yawned again. "Did you say Mauricio agreed to your bus tour?"

"That's what I said. So it looks like you'll be tracking down some-one's parents today."

She let out a pained sigh. "I love you and hate you right now. Tell me, how did you convince Mauricio to go with you?"

"I asked him."

"Really? You told him where you were going, and he thought it was a great idea?"

I paused. "Not exactly. I told him my plans, asked him to join me, and he agreed with the condition that he could plan tomorrow."

"And you said yes to that?"

Oh my God. "I didn't say no. I did warn him, though, that I'm pretty boring usually. Should I call him back and clarify that I didn't make any kind of binding agreement with him?"

Cecile laughed. "Please don't. Let me think this through. He prob-ably thinks he's pretty smooth. My guess is he'll try to end your tour early. Maybe even after the first stop. Don't let him. Right now you have the upper hand. Keep it. I bet most women don't make him work very hard for sex. Men like a challenge. Play hard to get, even if you want to jump him."

"I don't play games, Cecile. Isn't honesty always the best policy?"

She groaned again. "Almost never. And didn't you tell me you haven't had great sex so far?"

Touché. Look at me, already thinking in French. "What does that have to do with being up-front with someone?"

"Making yourself a challenge is what makes it exciting for a man. Don't think of that as a lie or a game; think of it as a dance. The best partners don't tell each other what to do; they don't discuss who they danced with last; they discover each other by learning to move together. The chase, the flirtation, that's the music . . . You can dance without it, but why would you?"

I stood and walked to the mirror. Dancing was not a passion of mine. In preparation for a friend's themed wedding, I took ballroom lessons and failed miserably at it. The instructor said I needed to follow rather than lead. I've never been good at giving up control.

Was that why my relationships failed as well? I didn't let go. I needed to establish clear parameters, maintain control. No chase. No wild flirting.

No music.

Huh.

I dug some lip gloss out of my makeup bag and applied it. "Thanks, Cecile. You've given me something to think about."

"Wren?"

"Yes?"

"Be careful."

CHAPTER SEVEN

Mauricio

Even as I made my way to the bus ticket kiosk, I doubted we'd actually take the tour. She wanted to see me again. I understood the feeling well. I'd spent a restless night, wondering how long Wren would make me wait before she called. I didn't doubt for a moment that she would. Not after the way she'd kissed me back. Brief as it had been, it made her feelings for me clear.

I arrived at the kiosk a few minutes before nine and scanned the street for a sign of her. She'd left an impact on me. Not only could I remember exactly how she looked, smelled, and tasted, but I found it difficult to think about much else. I smiled as I pictured her peering at me—completely hidden by the side of the hot tub, except for those deep-blue eyes of hers.

I checked my phone for the time and frowned. When I looked up, she was directly in front of me, dressed in comfortable shoes, jeans, a T-shirt, and round mirrored sunglasses. Her long hair was swept back in a ponytail, and she had a water bottle in each hand.

I automatically accepted the one she held out to me. The brush of her hand against mine was enough to send my thoughts scattering. She smiled brightly, and all I could think about was kissing those sweet lips of hers.

With her free hand she took a map from the side of the kiosk. "So, open top or closed?"

"Open," I replied automatically, then shook my head when I realized she was referring to the types of bus and not the scene my mind had wandered to again.

"I prefer those too," she said cheerfully, then stepped up to the window and ordered two passes. Over her shoulder, she asked, "I don't care if we go into any of the sights today. I just want to walk around, get my bearings, buy a few souvenirs, sit in a café, and sip strong coffee." Before I could get my own wallet out, she'd paid for both of us. When she turned back to me, she waved the tickets. "I asked you, so this is my treat."

She stepped away from the window and held out a ticket to me. I accepted it and took a moment to read it over. *We're actually doing this?* "Had I known you wanted to see the city, I would have hired a car."

Amusement lit her eyes. "I told you what my plans were for the morning."

"You did." Not even sure why, I smiled back. When was the last time my heart had beaten so wildly I found it difficult to concentrate? This thing between us—it was heady. *Lead away, Wren.*

Our eyes met and held for an electric moment. The pull of her was nearly irresistible. I leaned in, but just as I did, she whipped open a map. "It looks like from here we'll go around the Arc de Triomphe. I want to go to the observation level, but that can wait until later in the week. That area is close enough to walk to, so no stress there. The next stop is Trocadéro. It looks like it's right across the street from the Eiffel Tower. The blogs say the view is incredible from the top of the steps. I also want to walk around the tower. There are security checks to get beneath it, so we don't have to go in that area, but I'd like to. I've heard the lines for the tower are crazy if we don't have advance tickets, but we could still stroll around. What do you think?"

Her enthusiasm was so pure, I couldn't look away. With my index finger, I gently tipped her chin up so our eyes met again. Her lips parted, and I couldn't resist. I ran my lips gently over hers—a light, teasing kiss.

Her lips moved against mine in a caress that shot fire through me. When I raised my head, I said, "I'm in."

I was.

I would have agreed to go anywhere. I couldn't explain the strength of my attraction, but I definitely wasn't going to leave her side when being with her felt so good.

She looked away after our kiss, and her cheeks took on a pink hue. It was so sweet I wanted to hug her to me and promise we'd take this at whatever pace she needed. She busied herself with putting the map into her purse, then said, "Looks like we wait for the bus over there."

I offered her my hand.

She hesitated, and I held my breath. Not since grade school had I put so much stock into such an innocent gesture. I had no idea if she would take my hand or not.

The bus pulled up, and people pushed in around us, jostling to get on the bus first. In the mix, her hand found mine, and a huge grin spread across my face. I guided her onto the bus, reluctantly breaking off our connection to accept a pair of earbuds. We made our way up the stairs to the second level, a journey that provided me with a nice view of her rounded ass. Perfection.

She chose a spot in the middle on the right side. I sat beside her. What looked like a cruise tour filled the seats in front of us—loud, excited, and mostly American. Couples of varied ages and nationalities were scattered around, as well as a few single passengers. I was probably the only passenger sporting a woody, but I couldn't convince my cock that Wren wasn't deliberately trying to excite it. Each time she shifted to look down at the street, her thigh slid along mine. When she stood to watch the people still loading below, her ass was eye level and so perfectly rounded I looked away and chuckled at how being around her reduced me to a teenage version of myself.

The bus pulled out into traffic, and she sat beside me with a happy sigh. "Perfect weather. Great company." She waved her hands. "And freaking Paris!"

Her earbuds flew out of her hand and dropped to my feet. She instantly bent and began hunting for them, her face bobbing over my lap. It was too easy to imagine her there for an entirely different reason. In a strangled tone, I said, "I'll find them." I tossed her my unopened pair.

As I hunted around near my feet for the elusive little fuckers, I glanced up at her. She was in the process of choosing the correct channel for the audio tour. I've been with a lot of women—a lot. Too many, according to my brothers. Along the way, I'd gotten more than a little jaded. If things didn't work out with a woman, there was always another one ready to step in, just as eager to be with me.

This was so different it felt dangerous. I closed my hand around the earbuds and straightened. "Got them."

She nodded. Her eyes dilated, and she appeared as affected by me as I was by her.

Why were we on a tour and not in my bed? "Do you know what they have near Trocadéro?"

She shook her head without speaking.

"*Taxis,*" I said with sensual confidence.

She wrinkled her nose. "Do you know what else is there?"

"What?" I whispered, leaning closer.

"The Eiffel Tower." After shooting me a sexy little smile, she turned and pointed at the Arc de Triomphe as we passed it. "Can you believe Napoleon never saw the arc completed? He promised his soldiers they would walk through it, but he was defeated before it was completed. Twelve avenues lead to it, each named after a French military leader. Imagine the planning that went into making it happen. The architects who designed it are long gone, and forgotten by most people, but what they designed lives on. It tells a story of history so well, it has made its own mark." Her hands clasped on her lap. "I used to dream that I'd one day create something that would make a difference."

I placed my arm along the back of her chair. She sounded a little like she was spouting something she'd memorized from a guidebook. It made me wonder if traveling was new to her. There was such yearning in her last statement that I had to ask, "Are you an artist?"

"Engineer," she said with a shrug, as if that were a common thing. It wasn't, at least not in my circle of friends. I knew far too many people who hadn't had to work for what they had. They lacked the kind of strength I sensed in this woman. "I've always enjoyed learning how things work. I get that from my father." Her expression seemed conflicted—as if that fact made her both proud and a little sad. "What do you do?"

I didn't want to talk about me. There was so much more I wanted to know about her, but she was waiting for a response, so I said, "Until recently I helped run my family's company. Currently, I'm weighing my options. Deciding if that's what I want to continue to do."

She nodded. "Are you close to your family?"

"Very."

"Me too." There it was, that conflicted look again.

I took a guess and said, "It's not easy to balance family and career."

"No, it's not." Her voice lowered as she said, "I'm also at a bit of a crossroads, myself. That's why I'm here. I needed a little distance."

Her words resonated with me.

Crossroads.

I knew that place well.

A wisp of her hair blew across her eyes. I tucked it behind her ear. Touching her felt so natural. "Sometimes it helps to get an outside opinion."

"Does it?" Her tone was a light challenge.

I like women, but I don't normally delve too deeply into their lives. Things went smoother, ended easier, when exchanges were kept light. I surprised myself by saying, "I believe so."

She held my gaze for a long moment. "Ever feel like you were meant for more?" Her smile twisted with self-deprecation. "What do they call that? A false sense of grandeur?"

I traced the line of her neck with my thumb. "I suppose that depends on what you mean by more."

She cocked her head to one side. "I'm not looking for fame or money. I just want to do something important." She looked down at her hands before meeting my gaze again. "I stayed in my hometown so I could be close to my parents. I have a good life there. I should be happy, but . . . is it wrong to also want some of this?" She waved a hand at the city that was a blur behind her.

"I don't think so." I wanted more of *this*—her beside me, openly sharing. "You don't think you could have both?"

She let out a shaky breath. "I don't know. Sometimes I do, but then I worry that if I look away from my family for a moment . . ." Her voice trailed off, and she bit her bottom lip.

"What would happen?" My voice was barely above a whisper, but she heard me.

The tears that filled her eyes hit me like a sucker punch. She opened her mouth as if about to tell me, then shook her head without uttering a word. She turned away again and exclaimed, "Oh, look. The Trocadéro. Gorgeous."

Yes. She was.

I was tangled up on the inside . . . protective of the innocence she exuded and turned on more than I should be. Wren wasn't the kind of woman who should be with a man like me. She was the type my parents were praying all their sons would one day settle down with. Sebastian had found Heather. Intelligent. Unpretentious. Sweet. Trusting. Wren was the same.

Completely the wrong choice for a one-night stand.

Listening to Wren made me wish I were a different kind of man. Cecile had warned me not to break her friend's heart. I'd dismissed the warning, but it echoed in my head as I looked down at Wren. People liked me too much, too fast. Would she?

Her devotion to her family had shone in her eyes. Someone like that probably fell hard.

I wanted to be with her, but I didn't want to hurt her.

Or live through the guilt that would follow.

For all my superficial gifts, or perhaps because of them, I wasn't capable of love.

Lust? Absolutely.

Sustained interest in one woman? It had never happened.

If she fell for me, she'd be devastated when I lost interest. And I would. Sure this was intense, but that didn't mean the feeling would last. She didn't come across as someone who was experienced enough to realize that.

I needed to end the date early—before I gave in to the temptation of her.

The bus pulled over.

She chuckled and twirled her earbuds in the air. "We didn't even use them. Oh, well, hang on to yours. We can use them when we hop back on."

Several of the people around us had begun to make their way toward the stairs. I stood and took out my phone. "I should check in with my office—"

Her expression fell as she rose as well. "Of course."

She knew I was about to cut out, and her disappointment was clear. I'd already done what I was trying to avoid—taken the sparkle out of her eyes. Better this way, though, than to break her heart later. "I'm in Paris on business. I wanted to see you, but . . ."

"But you don't want to fuck me enough to stay for the whole tour. I get it. Just go."

"Whoa, what?" *Did I hear her right?*

The bus pulled out into traffic again, taking us both unawares. Over the intercom, in multiple languages, the driver requested that everyone remain seated.

She sat down with a huff and took out her map again. "Great, we missed the stop. The next one is farther down the river near the *bateaux-mouches*. I guess I could circle back . . . or take one of those."

Speaking of circling back. I sat down again, turning to face her. "What did you just say?"

"The *bateaux-mouches*. They're a kind of boat."

"I know what *bat*—before that. About me not wanting you enough to stay for the tour?"

Before answering, she folded the map up and stuffed it in her pocket. "Cecile predicted you'd ditch and run after the first stop. Actually, she doubted you'd even agree to come on the tour at all. That was the bet we had. She said today would be a good gauge of how much you wanted to be with me."

My eyebrows headed toward my hairline. Wren was a strange mix of shy and blunt. "So this was a test."

She looked down, then met my eyes again. "For her, not for me. I thought it would be fun to spend the day with you. Sadly, you lived down to her expectations. So it's fine. Get off at the next stop. I didn't come to Paris to meet anyone." She glared at me. "All you're doing now is blocking my view."

She crossed her arms and turned away from me.

I stared at the back of her head for a time, then folded my arms as well and sat back. No good deed goes unpunished. There I was trying to do the right thing, trying to be the good guy for once, and what did it get me?

Dismissed.

Neither of us spoke. A silent standoff.

She shot me an irritated look as she put in her earbuds.

Childishly, I did the same, even though I couldn't have cared less about the Paris information on the recording.

When the bus stopped near the river, I didn't get up. If she wanted me to move, she could damn well ask me to.

She didn't. She sat there, earbuds still in, back to me, as if I were a stranger she was barely tolerating.

The tour announced the next stop would be directly in front of the Eiffel Tower. She'd been so excited about walking around it. I couldn't let her miss it. I took out my earbuds and touched her arm.

She removed hers and gave me such a cold look I smiled. Right or wrong, I liked that she wasn't worried about impressing me.

Her eyes narrowed. "Yes?"

What I should do and what I wanted to do were in direct opposition to each other. Was there a third option, one that included bringing the smile back to her eyes without taking things too far? "I've never walked around the Eiffel Tower."

"No?" She didn't sound like she believed me.

"No. I spent a good deal of time in Paris when I was younger, but mostly at clubs."

She glanced at me, then turned to look forward. "I can see that."

I wasn't used to being dismissed. I ducked to speak closer to her ear. "Can you? VIP everything. Never waiting in line—ever. I was kind of a big deal in this city."

The look she gave me made me replay my words in my head, then groan. She was not impressed, and I couldn't blame her. I was acting like an idiot. My brain didn't function right around her.

She arched an eyebrow. "It doesn't sound like we have anything in common. I'd rather skip the line at a museum than a bar."

I wanted to say, "Me too," but I couldn't remember the last time I'd been inside a museum. Grade school field trip? No, wait, I'd also gone to one as part of a college assignment. Her expression hardened the longer I remained silent.

She looked me over again, then said, "I don't care how boring it sounds or if I've offended you. Usually I would. I spend too much time worrying about how everyone else feels and making sure they're all okay. I'm on vacation from that, and this is my first time in Europe. I refuse to apologize for wanting to see everything—and that includes all the touristy sights as well as any hidden gems I come across. So stay or go. I really don't care."

I wasn't offended—I was impressed.

I liked the way she knew exactly what she wanted. People often weren't honest with me. They hid their flaws, lied about their preferences, did what I wanted to do. I'd gotten used to it—had come to accept it as normal. Wren was proof that some people were made of tougher stuff. What did that say about the women I'd chosen to be with?

For several years, keeping Sebastian out of trouble and my family's company afloat had been all-consuming. Perhaps easy was all I could handle back then. But how about now? I had my freedom again. What did I want to do with it?

The idea of heading back into the clubs wasn't tempting. Returning to a city where I'd once run so wild had clarified that point for me. I didn't want to go back. I wanted to move forward . . . I also didn't want my time with Wren to end yet. "Wren, I want to see Paris with you— your way." As I said the words, I realized how much I meant them.

She searched my face, not yet looking as if she fully believed me. "I would say something witty, but I'm not good at flirting."

I fought a smile. "We could work on that."

Her eyes narrowed again, but I could also see that my comment had amused her. "And just to get this out there, if anything does happen between us—you are absolutely wearing a condom."

"Absolutely." I coughed back a laugh. Never had I found anyone as funny as Wren, even though she wasn't trying to be.

The bus pulled over again. I stood and held out my hand for her to take. "Let's go see the Eiffel Tower."

She rose and her eyes lit with challenge. "There are over twenty stops on this tour."

"Sounds like fun."

She placed her hand in mine, and we made our way through the bus and to the street. Once there, I pulled her closer and bent to growl in her ear. "Wanting to end the tour had nothing to do with how interested I am in you, but now that I know what you're determining from today—hang on to your water bottle, pumpkin, because we'll ride that bus until you're begging to stop."

Her expression showed her surprise.

I swooped in for a quick kiss that left me feeling as rattled as she'd looked. I could have fucked her right there; that was how strong the sizzle between us was. The intense kind of euphoria that made the sky look as blue as her eyes and the sunshine feel brighter.

My resolve to protect her from me battled with my desire for her. My body was overheating, and my thoughts were a hot mess—and it was fucking incredible. I put my arm around her waist and turned her so she'd have a view of the Eiffel Tower. "So, my little engineer, tell me something I don't know about this icon."

CHAPTER EIGHT

WREN

My mind raced as I tried to focus on the iron landmark before us. Part of me wanted to tell Mauricio to stop kissing me. Another part wanted to turn, wrap my arms around his neck, and beg him to kiss me again.

How could I be expected to form a coherent sentence while trying to sort it out?

I pretended to be momentarily overwhelmed by the Eiffel Tower, but really I was catching my breath and trying to regain my composure. I groaned inwardly as I remembered how I'd blurted out that being with me required using protection. In my head, it had sounded sophisticated and sexy. If Mauricio's amusement was anything to go by, it hadn't come across as either.

Yet he was still at my side.

He didn't have to be. I'd told him he could go.

My cheeks warmed as I remembered how he'd promised to ride the bus until I begged to stop. What else would he do with that kind of dedication?

What did it say that I wanted to find out?

My very responsible life was waiting for me back in Connecticut. If I didn't share our time on social media, no one back home would even know about my time with him. It wouldn't affect my parents or my job. He was my chance to walk on the wild side before stepping back into my life.

So tempting, how could I resist?

I glanced around, and although the area was full of all types of people my attention was drawn by young couples displaying public affection for each other. Some sat together on the grass. Some kissed in the middle of the crowd, seemingly oblivious that they were not alone. They made it look so easy.

I realized Mauricio was waiting for me to say something. He wasn't the type to go to museums. Did he really want to hear what I knew about the tower? Even as I asked myself the question, I squared my shoulders and reminded myself that this trip was about not worrying for a change. If he didn't like hearing historical facts, no one was forcing him to stay. "The story of the Eiffel Tower is fascinating. It was built to show France's industrial prowess for a world fair. The plan was to tear it down after twenty years. Part of the original contest to design it actually included a caveat that it must be easy to dismantle. Imagine three hundred men, over two years, eighteen thousand thirty-eight pieces of wrought iron held together with two-and-a-half million rivets, all for something that was meant to be temporary."

A couple walked by us, pausing to kiss passionately. The young woman whispered something in her lover's ear that brought a grin to his face before they hurried off together.

I wasn't positive, but my gut hinted what she'd whispered hadn't been the history of the Eiffel Tower. I groaned inwardly. Was I playing this wrong? My sex life was a snore fest . . . did I want it to stay that way?

A gorgeous man was literally holding my hand. He'd already made it clear he wanted me. All I had to do was get out of my own way and let it happen.

I glanced up at Mauricio, half expecting to see his eyes glassed over and him reaching for his phone again. The warm smile he gave me sent fire licking through me.

He dipped his head closer to mine. "So why does it remain?"

"What?" Did I mention how dark his eyes were? His perfect white teeth? How solid and strong every inch of him was? My heart thudded crazily in my chest, and I became acutely aware of every single place our bodies were touching.

"They obviously didn't tear the tower down. Do you know why?"

I shook my head. Why were we talking about a metal structure when my body was literally humming for his?

His smile widened. "I'm surprised. I was sure you'd know."

I blinked a few times quickly. "About why the Eiffel Tower is still standing?"

Desire burned in his eyes as they searched my face. "Yes. So many things don't last. Why is it still here?"

It was difficult to breathe, even harder to concentrate when he looked at me that way. I flicked my tongue across my bottom lip. "It's complicated. When it was first built, it was considered ugly. To protect it, Eiffel proved it could be useful for science and as a radio transmitter. So it survived its demolition date. Later, when the Nazis took Paris, the French cut the cables, which meant the Nazis had to climb one thousand seven hundred ten steps to hang their victory flag from it, and the first one was so big it blew off. They had to climb back up and hang a much smaller flag. The tower would not be humbled. There's a beauty when something survives in spite of what others expect of it. I can't speak for Parisians, but that's why I think they embrace it now. Not because of its lights or its global popularity, but because it's an emotional symbol of French resilience. Despite all odds, it still stands." I stopped because I felt like I was rambling. "Sorry, did that answer your question?"

"Yes." He traced the line of my chin with his thumb and looked down into my eyes without speaking for several heartbeats. "And no. I've never met anyone like you, Wren."

I swallowed hard. "That's a good thing, right?" I joked.

His answer was a kiss that had me twining myself around him. There might have been people around us. It could have still been daylight. None of that mattered. His hands dug into my hair. I went up onto my tiptoes, kissing him back with abandon.

When he broke off the kiss, he rested his forehead against mine. "You've been up-front with me, so it's only fair that I be as well. I want to be with you, but I don't want to hurt you. I'm not good at relationships. If you're looking for forever, you won't find it with me."

Our breath mingled intimately as I weighed his words. He wasn't looking for anything long term. Another woman might have been disappointed, but I wasn't good at relationships either. No matter how good they started, there was a pattern to how mine ended. I had yet to find a man who understood that my parents would always be a priority to me. I didn't want to move away from them. Nor did I need to be saved from the situation.

The men I'd dated had wanted to be number one in my life. I didn't love like that. The man I wanted wouldn't see my parents as competition. He'd understand that even the weight of such a responsibility was a gift. The possibility that such a man might not exist was not something I wanted to waste time lamenting. Mauricio was offering something temporary, and in a way it was a bit of a relief. I didn't need to worry about what a vacation fling thought of my life choices, or if he would blend well with my parents. No, I could concentrate solely on this sizzle and how good it felt to be wanted by a gorgeous man.

"I'm not looking for forever. How about we just have some fun?"

"Some fun." He echoed my words as if doubting my claim.

I ran my hands up his strong chest. God, he felt good. "I want to be with you, too, and I'm willing to shoulder whatever guilt comes with breaking your heart."

"You are?" he asked in a deep, amused voice.

"I am. I'm only here for a week, so don't let yourself get too attached."

He raised his head and looked down at me with desire burning in his eyes. "What am I going to do with you?"

Inspiration hit me, and I pulled his head down so I could whisper, "Something so decadent I fly home smiling."

His eyes widened, his hard cock twitched against my stomach, and he growled, "I like the way you think."

I moved slowly, experimentally back and forth against his erection, reveling in the guttural groan the action elicited from him. "And I like the way you feel."

He claimed my mouth again, this time plundering it as if I'd pushed him beyond gentleness. I loved the way his hands tightened in my hair, loved how he took control of the kiss. Had we not been in public I doubted our clothing would have stayed on long.

Eventually we broke off the kiss and simply held each other, both breathing heavily. His voice was husky when he asked, "So what's the next stop on the tour?"

Was he serious, or was this where I was supposed to say his place? I didn't know. During my hesitation, he added, "My guess is it's Hôtel des Invalides."

Hotel.

No, not a hotel like its name implied, but a complex of buildings where Napoleon I was buried. I needed to calm down. That might require fresh air and stepping out of Mauricio's embrace. "You're right. I'd like to walk around here first, though."

Or find a real hotel . . .

No, there was no need to rush that.

And I really did want to see Paris.

Mauricio tucked some of my hair back in place, then stepped back. "Keep telling me what you want, Wren, because you've given me a goal . . . to send you home smiling."

My mouth went dry. "It's good to have goals."

"Yes, it is." He put his arm around my waist, and we began to walk the perimeter of the tower. When we approached a security entrance, he asked, "Still sure you don't want to go inside?"

I scanned the area inside and the long lines of people that filled it. "Not today. We'd need tickets to go up. I'll come back."

I'd almost said, "We can come back," but I had no idea if we would.

We strolled along, hand in hand. Each time I glanced up at him and caught him watching me, I smiled, blushed, and looked away. I felt young and sexy, and the whole day felt like a dream. "Tell me something you've never told anyone," I challenged spontaneously.

His hand gave mine a light squeeze, and he pulled me closer as we walked. "Something I've never told anyone. Let's see. I can't watch *The Wizard of Oz* because I don't like the—"

"Flying monkeys?" I cut in with my guess.

He nodded.

"Me too. They gave me nightmares as a child. And in *Willy Wonka and the Chocolate Factory* it was the—"

"Oompa-Loompas," he interjected with a laugh.

We shared a smile. "Anything stuck in Jell-O freaks me out—even fruit."

"If I chase a spider with a shoe and he gets away, I have trouble sleeping because I'm positive he's plotting his revenge."

I chuckled at that. "I always look under the bed of a hotel room. I've never found anyone, but I watched too many horror movies in my teens to trust there is no one there."

"Thanks, now I'm going to wonder until I check. I have another. I'd like to visit my cousins in Montalcino, but I'm not ready to get married."

My eyebrows rose. "You plan on marrying one of your cousins?"

"Oh God, no." Thankfully he sounded as put off by the idea as I'd been. "That sounded bad, didn't it? My nonna thinks we're all too old to be single. Sebastian visited her last year and said she'd arranged for him to meet every available woman in miles."

I brought my free hand to my heart, and this time my shock was for dramatic effect. "How awful. I hope he made it out alive. Who's Sebastian?"

He shook his head in amusement. "My oldest brother." We stopped and he tapped a finger on my nose in light reprimand. "I didn't mock your fear of fruit in Jell-O."

Yes, but who could fear a matchmaking grandmother? That sounded adorable. "How many siblings do you have?"

We moved to sit on a bench in the sunshine. "Three brothers. One older and two younger. How about you?"

"It's just me and my parents," I said, forcing a bright smile and looking at our laced hands. "But I'd love a litter of children."

"A litter? How many is that?"

If Mauricio and I had met in the United States, and I thought there was any chance that we might have turned serious, I would have worried that the truth would scare him off. He'd already told me he didn't do forever. Hell, he might not even do tomorrow. There was a freedom in that knowledge. I could be myself—the Paris vacation version of myself, anyway. "At least three. Maybe five. I had a nice childhood, but I was often alone. I wanted someone to fight for the bathroom with, someone to stay up too late giggling with. My friends had love/hate relationships with their brothers and sisters, and I envied that." I glanced at Mauricio. "Is this where you tell me siblings are overrated?"

His eyes darkened with an emotion I couldn't discern. "Not at all. I can't imagine not having my brothers in my life. We're all different, but if something happens to one of us, we're there for each other."

"That's what I want for my children," I said simply. "It's not easy to shoulder everything myself."

He nodded, and we were quiet for a moment. "Are your parents unwell?"

Once again, on a normal first date that wasn't something I would have shared. This was about feeling good and having fun. If I could also squeeze a little therapy session out of it? Well, what was the harm? "Yes and no. My mother was cleaning houses, but it became too physically challenging as she got older. My father"—it felt good to talk about what my family refused to back home—"he was an engineer in the army, and a good one. Didn't matter what it was, he could design it, fix it, or pinpoint a weakness so it could be destroyed. Everyone thought he would invent something revolutionary. At least, that's what his army buddies tell me. I never knew that side of him. He was injured in an IED accident, lost his right arm, and left the military. After that he opened a gas station in my hometown. Not much money in it, but he's independent. Mostly independent."

There was a surprising amount of understanding in Mauricio's eyes. "And you stayed nearby to be available when your parents need you."

No judgment.

No declaration that I shouldn't.

He understood in a way I hadn't expected him to. "Yes. They've done everything for me, made sure I always had what I needed. I'm happy to help out in any way I can." Wait, while I was being honest . . . "I just wish I could be two people."

He leaned in. "Now I'm intrigued. The woman I'm getting to know seems wonderful in her own right. Who else do you wish you could be?"

I glanced around and took a moment. Despite the fact that we were holding hands, Mauricio wasn't what mattered most about my trip to Paris. The question he'd asked was. It was the same one I'd asked myself so many times lately. What was my life missing? "Doing the right thing is supposed to be its own reward, isn't it? I should be happier than I am. I'm looking for something . . . I just haven't figured out what yet."

"I understand that feeling."

I scanned his face for any hint he might be tiring of the conversation but found only compassion. Funny, he was out of my league in the looks department—truly, he belonged on the big screen while I happily blended in with most crowds—but it didn't feel that way. What was he doing with me, and why wasn't he a conceited ass?

Just then I remembered what Cecile had said about him. Mauricio was the type who would sell a woman the fantasy . . . sweep a woman off her feet . . . then not know her name. I expected the sweeping part to be tacky and easy to dismiss. His sustained attention, the way he really seemed to care—a woman could get addicted to fantasy.

The challenge would be to remember it wasn't real.

"If I could be two people . . ." I gave myself over to a playful idea. "I'd be myself and a wild sex kitten."

Unfortunately, as I finished the sentence, a group of loud children had passed by, and I wasn't sure he'd heard it. My eyes flew to his. Nothing. He'd missed it.

I swallowed hard.

Did I dare say it again?

He dipped his head a little closer, bringing his ear to just a few inches from my mouth. "Sorry?"

I took a deep breath, and in a loud whisper, I said, "Myself. I'd be my practical self, and I'd also be a wild sex kitten."

"I missed that last part."

I pulled back, ready to say it again louder. Then I saw the teasing sparkle in his eyes. "Asshole."

A grin spread across his face. "Kitten."

Embarrassment and desire flooded me in equal parts. I started to pull my hand free from his. "Don't make fun of me."

His fingers tightened on mine, and he placed my hand on his thigh. "Never."

My breath caught in my throat. Our connection felt so real. "What are you doing with me?" I hadn't meant to voice the question, and certainly not in the earnest tone I'd used.

He ran my hand a little farther up his thigh, almost to where, oh God, the evidence of how much he was enjoying our time together was right there in bulging glory. "The better question would be, What are *you* doing with me? You seem to know what you want. So tell me, Kitten, what do you want *from me?*"

Oh yes, because he deals in fantasies. At least he's willing to craft mine to my specifications. I thought about my prior relationships. None of them had been very exciting. Did I dare share that? I took a moment to describe my own part in how unexciting my sex life had been. "Back home, I'm often one of the guys. Nothing magical ever happens . . . men don't see me as someone to romance. For just a couple days, I want to wear crazy-small underwear, sip champagne on a balcony, kiss on the steps of Montmartre, see the sights, then . . ."

"Then," he prompted with a smile that was pure sin.

I shifted my hand up his thigh on my own. My smile was a challenge and a promise. "If you can't figure out the next part, I've chosen the wrong date."

His kiss was the answer my body craved. It was bold and skilled. The crowd disappeared and time slowed until there was only this man and how good his lips felt on mine. When his tongue dipped into my mouth, I met it eagerly.

By the time he lifted his head, we were both breathing raggedly. "You chose right. How long are you in Paris?"

I could barely remember my name—and he wanted my itinerary? "I fly back Saturday."

"Me too."

He didn't ask if I wanted to travel back with him because our time together had an expiration date. Normally that would bother me, but I was in Paris, and at twenty-seven I was a hop, skip, and a jump from turning thirty without ever doing anything crazy. One day, God willing, I'd be living a simple life, happily married with kids. When my daughters asked me if I'd ever done anything wild, I wanted to be able to lie and say I hadn't.

I didn't want my denial to be the truth.

I met Mauricio's gaze and shivered with pleasure at the hunger I saw there. "Do you have any plans between now and then?" he asked in a deep, oh-so-smooth tone.

I bit my bottom lip before answering, "It's still mostly up in the air."

He bent near my ear. "Then consider yourself mine until Saturday."

I nearly stood and stripped right there. *I'm in.*

A little voice in my head warned that I should clarify what being "his" meant before agreeing, but when he kissed me again, I decided we could sort the details out as we went.

CHAPTER NINE

MAURICIO

I'd told myself to take it slowly with Wren.

I needed to stop kissing her before I dragged her off to the bushes and we got arrested for doing any of the things I was imagining. I sat back and put my arm across the bench behind her, striving to look less affected by her than I was.

Consider yourself mine until Saturday . . .

She hadn't said yes, but she sure as hell hadn't said no.

She should have said no.

It wasn't that I'd never been with a woman who would have agreed to a temporary arrangement. In fact, five days would be more commitment than most hookups would want. By my standards, breakfast in the morning was overkill. Nothing worse than a lingering lay. Chop-chop, ladies. Everyone had places to go, and showering at my place never made a repeat performance more likely.

Sure, that made me sound like a dick, but I chose women with similar philosophies. I'd never expected anyone to make *me* breakfast. Morning sex? Sure, if I woke up and my date was still there and we both had time. But anything more would have been unnecessary pretense.

So why the hell had I promised a woman I just met almost a week of my time?

I rolled my eyes skyward.

Come on, what man could turn down a sex kitten wannabe? How could I be expected to not put time into that tutorial?

Time was relative. Five days of sitting through meetings with Felix would have dragged on. Helping Wren find her wild side? That would fly by.

I glanced down at her. She gave me that shy smile of hers that made me want to hug her as much as I wanted to fuck her. She was looking for romance from a man who didn't do romance—who'd never had to.

What did men do when they wanted to woo a woman?

The more I thought about it, though, the more I liked the idea of flexing that muscle. Others had called me amazing without asking me to put much effort in. Wren wanted magic. The idea of giving her that memory, of sending her home with a huge, satisfied grin on her face, was exciting.

I'm going to rock this woman's world.

I'll show her the perks of being with a man who knows his way around a woman's body.

She already looked willing to end the tour early. I could have stolen her away somewhere private, but I didn't want to—not yet.

Why?

The answer was somewhere in that sweet smile of hers. I didn't want to just fuck her. Didn't want to just wow her. This was a woman who cared for her parents. Earnest. Confident enough to be here and to have been clear about what she wanted, but innocent enough to make me wonder if every man in her hometown was blind.

I didn't want her to regret her time with me.

I glanced back at the road, where a large red open-topped bus was passing by. I'd also vowed to ride that thing until she begged for it to end. Taking her hand once again in mine, I stood. "Ready to continue the tour, Kitten?"

She rose to her feet and met my gaze. "I *do* want to see Paris."

I laughed. "So do I." Five days. No need to rush. I would take my time and savor the anticipation. Even if that involved spending the day on a crowded bus.

Inspiration sparked her eyes and she leaned in. "Do you speak French?"

"A little."

She bit her bottom lip. "How do you say *kitten* in French? Maybe you could call me that."

I coughed on a laugh. "Not a good idea. In French the word for a kitten or female cat is usually a reference to a part of you I can't pet in public."

"Oh. Wow. Right. English then." Her face went pink.

"In public at least," I murmured.

She looked down, then met my gaze again. "Only because I'd hate to see you arrested."

I laughed. She might not think she was a good flirt, but everything she did and said was proving effective at keeping my cock in a constant, painful state of arousal.

I placed my hand on her back, and we started to walk. My phone rang. I reluctantly answered. "Speak."

"I'm getting discharged around noon. Is Cecile out?"

"I believe so. We didn't discuss a time."

"What did you tell her?"

"What you told me to."

"Are you with someone? Is that why you can't speak?"

"That is correct."

"Anyone I know?"

"Better not be." I looked Wren over again and a wave of jealousy took me by surprise. If Felix hadn't broken his favorite appendage, he would have been the one to meet Wren while she was in the hot tub with Cecile. Was that the kind of wild she was looking for? I didn't like that I didn't know. Normally I was fine sharing, but the idea of another man's or woman's mouth tasting hers filled me with . . . a possessive anger I hadn't known I was capable of.

Mine. Even if only for five days. I ended the call and spun Wren so she was in my arms on the side of the path. "From now until Saturday there is no one else."

Her eyes widened, then lit with more amusement than was flattering. "So, super-short-term monogamy. I can handle that."

I was self-aware enough to understand why she was laughing at me. It sounded ridiculous, but I needed to know that no one else would have her. "Good."

The kiss I gave her was rougher than I meant it to be. I plundered; I claimed. My hands dug into her hair, and I ground my lips against hers. No, it didn't make sense, but this attraction went to a primal level.

When I raised my head, I half expected her to push me away. Never had I felt so close to losing control. Instead she ran one of her fingers lightly over her swollen bottom lip. She flicked the end of it with her tongue before raising that wet finger to trace my lips.

I took it gently between my teeth and held it.

A shudder passed through her body. "If you want—"

"Not yet." I knew what she was offering, but that was not how I wanted this to go. It wasn't what she wanted either, not really. "First I want to prove to you just how much I want you."

She shifted against my swollen cock. "I have a pretty good idea."

I chuckled, then bent down and said, "If you want to see Paris, I suggest we do it before I get you in my bed. Something tells me once I have you there, neither of us will want much else."

"Crepes," she said breathlessly.

I shook my head in confusion.

"Sex makes me hungry, and I've always wanted to try the crepes here." She said it so openly, so matter-of-factly, that I threw back my head and laughed.

"Condoms and crepes. I'm making a list, Kitten."

Her gaze fell to my chest. "And maybe a toy."

Whoosh, that knocked the breath clear out of me. "Really?"

Without looking up, she continued, "Nothing too crazy, I've just always wanted to try one."

I hugged her. Could she hear my heart beating crazily in my chest? "How have you not used one?"

She mumbled, "I was always afraid someone would know. Aren't they noisy?"

I kissed the top of her head and chuckled. "We'll find you a quiet one." I reluctantly stepped back. "Come on, I see the next bus coming."

We got to the stop just in time. A moment later we were seated once again in the open top level. This time my arm stayed around her.

"So the call you had earlier—was it Felix?"

I might not be the forever kind of guy, but I've also never been a liar. I couldn't say it had been Felix on the phone. Doing so might open the door to questions I wouldn't be able to answer without betraying Felix.

She frowned. "You don't have to tell me. I can see it on your face. Where is he? With another woman?"

All I could do was look at her and remind myself I was following the only protocol I could, considering my friend had broken his dick.

She looked away, then turned toward me with fire in her eyes. "Just to be clear, I don't care if we last a day or a week, don't ever send someone to tell me to leave. You should both be ashamed of yourselves for treating Cecile that way."

I opened my mouth and didn't like how my first response sounded too much like I was defending myself, so I snapped it shut again.

Without knowing what Felix was going through, my role the night before appeared callous. Even a one-night stand deserved more respect than it looked like we'd given Cecile. I sighed. "Tell Cecile it wasn't Felix's intention to hurt her. He's dealing with something right now that he felt he needed to handle on his own."

"So he had you *handle* Cecile." Wren pursed her lips, then seemed to relax. "That didn't give me a great first impression of you."

I ran my hand over her hair. Yes, Wren wanted me, but she wasn't enamored of me. I wondered about the men she'd been with, and my mood soured. Had she imagined a future with any of them? Did she still think of them? *I bet she wanted to know their last names. She doesn't want to know mine.* "Then I'm glad I have the next few days to change your opinion of me."

She gave me an odd look. "Does it really matter what I think of you?"

Her question cut through me. I had voiced that exact question myself with other women, usually while bantering back and forth with one I didn't care if I saw again.

I hardly knew Wren, and I had no expectation of seeing her again after this week.

But I didn't like how okay she was with that scenario.

Which made no sense, but not much had since we'd met.

Her smile twisted as she apparently assigned her own meaning to my silence. "That's what I thought." She squared her shoulders. "And it's okay, because I don't want more than this."

Me either, I told myself.

CHAPTER TEN

WREN

Rather than getting off at the next stop, we rode through several. I put only one earbud in so I could hear the tour but also talk to Mauricio. Most of our conversation revolved around either a fun fact we'd learned from the audio tour or something beautiful we passed.

Our conversation had momentarily gone somewhere uncomfortable, and we'd both pulled back to the safety of superficial topics.

"Oh, let's get off here," I exclaimed as the bus stopped within a block of Paris's oldest section. If Mauricio hadn't quickly risen to his feet, I might very well have climbed over him. As soon as we hit the pavement, I spared him a smile. "Sorry, I love history and architecture. Have you been to the sister islands? Île de la Cité and Île Saint-Louis?"

Mauricio placed his hand on my lower back and shrugged. "I'm sure I have."

I checked my phone's GPS to make sure I knew which direction to head, and I stepped out onto a crosswalk. "I'm so excited."

Mauricio trotted to keep up with me. "I can see that."

"I read a blog that described the islands as a village within a city—a sliver of the seventeenth century that has been frozen in time. I want to walk on their narrow cobblestone streets. I want to stand on the point of Île Saint-Louis, where I can see Notre Dame and just soak in the history of it, even with the recent fire." We were crossing another busy street when our hands naturally intertwined. It was a little scary how comfortable I felt with a man I knew very little about. That concern fell away, though, as soon as we reached a main road that ran parallel to the Seine and the two islands came into view. Long covered boats, *bateaux-mouches*, slid by on the river. The stone wall of the islands reminded me of castles I'd dreamed of as a child.

Magical and romantic—just as I'd requested.

We made our way across the Pont de la Tournelle bridge. Tall stone-facade buildings lined the edge of the Île Saint-Louis, their endless rows of windows designed to give every resident a view of the river. The streets narrowed as we made our way toward the center of the island. I stopped in my tracks when I looked along the street that ran down the middle. Unlike so many other areas in Paris, it wasn't overcrowded. Boutique shops, bakeries, *fromageries*, and cafés lined both sides of the street. The sound of French being spoken created a musical background to my trip back in time. I gripped Mauricio's hand. "Love at first sight is a real thing."

"Excuse me?"

Sorry, Mauricio, but in this moment Paris has my heart. I touched the cornerstone of the nearest building. "I can feel the soul of the city here. Look, that cobblestone was laid hundreds of years ago. Before cars. Before computers, people stood here, looked down this very road, and saw shops just as we are. It hasn't changed with the rest of the world. It's like traveling back in time. Imagine taking a tiny island of farmland and not only making it residential, but also connecting it to the rest of the city in such a way that it becomes its heart. I get giddy just thinking about it. I've always read that Paris is the city of love, and now I see why they call it that."

"I doubt that was what they were referring to."

I pulled my gaze from the view of Rue Saint-Louis to see if his expression matched his dry tone. It did. I might have been blown away by the history before me, but he wasn't. How could he not be?

Oh, wait, because for him today was about building a fantasy. Disappointing, but important to remember. I already knew we had nothing in common. It had been foolish of me to expect him to get excited about the history of the island. I told myself not to, but I couldn't not ask him: "What do you see when you look down this road?"

"Is there something here besides you?" His smile was all practiced charm.

I frowned.

First I was irritated with him for being less than I wished he were.

Next I was irritated with myself for not being able to let go and simply enjoy my time with him. I hadn't had sex in years, and he was beautiful. If his cock was half as big as he seemed to think it was, it would be more satisfying than spending another night with my own hand. He didn't have bad breath. He might even know what he was doing in bed. Did it have to be more complicated than that?

"You're glaring at me." He tipped his head to the side and spoke slowly, as if this was something he hadn't encountered before.

I flexed my shoulders back and forth and tried to shake off my mood. "Sorry. I was just hoping you might share my enthusiasm. It's not important."

Now he was frowning. "It obviously is to you."

I didn't know how to respond to that, or if I was even supposed to, so I just held his gaze without speaking.

We stood that way for several long minutes . . . another silent standoff.

Great, I've made it awkward again.

He blinked first and ran his hand through his hair. "Sorry, I'm used to things being easier."

I rolled my eyes. "Because women normally throw themselves at your feet?"

"They aim higher, but yes."

My mouth rounded in shock; then I saw the smile in his eyes. "Charming."

"That's how they describe me."

"That's not the word that comes to my mind." I folded my arms across my chest.

A grin spread across his face. "Really. Care to share?"

"Cocky."

"What some call cocky others call confidence," he challenged, not looking at all bothered.

"Tell me, if you're so great, why aren't you in a relationship?"

"I told you I'm not good at them." He mirrored my stance. "Besides, I've never been in love."

"So you're always the one who ends it?"

His frown deepened. "Yes."

"But if you'd wanted more, any one of those women would have stayed with you?"

Oh, he didn't like that. "I didn't say that."

"But you think it."

This time Mauricio glared at me.

I took a mental step back from the scene and wanted to smack myself for killing the mood. What was wrong with me? Why was I angry? Mauricio was exactly who he claimed to be. He was being the charming, attentive Paris fling I'd said I was looking for.

It shouldn't matter how big his ego was or that he didn't care about the history of the island.

"Tell me, Wren, if you're so great, why aren't *you* in a relationship?"

My cheeks warmed, but before I had time to feel the sting of his question, he smiled. Have I mentioned how beautiful his smile was? It was the kind that could stop a woman in her tracks. Even me. "It could be my unfiltered mouth," I admitted, my own smile blooming.

He lowered his arms and leaned down until his breath tickled my lips. "No, your mouth is perfect."

So was his. I swallowed hard. "My obsession with engineering?"

His thumb traced my jaw, then the outline of my lips. "No, that's actually a turn-on."

"How judgmental I can be?" I whispered.

"Shut up and kiss me, Wren," he commanded.

I threw my arms around his neck and did just that. Right there on the corner of the street, I let myself go and kissed him with the hunger that had been building within me all day. Our bodies ground together. Our tongues danced. His hands gripped my hips. My hands ran wildly through his hair.

When he ended the kiss, we were both shaking. He tucked my head beneath his chin and hugged me to his chest as our ragged breathing slowly returned to normal. "Holy shit, Wren."

Still humming from our kiss, I let myself savor the feel of my cheek on his strong chest before I murmured, "I'm sorry about what I said. Can I claim jet lag brain? I don't normally insult my dates."

I felt as well as heard his chuckle. "No need to apologize. I'm the ass. My family would love you—they'd say you're exactly what I deserve."

My chest tightened. It would have been too easy to forget again that we had a set expiration date. Mauricio was certainly gifted at building the fantasy. I realized why I was angry—I was afraid I might not be able to stay emotionally uninvolved. With just a smile he could crack through my defenses.

And I needed those defenses.

I had responsibilities—a life without room for a man like this.

My hand fisted on his chest, and I slammed it against him. He encircled it. "Look at me, Kitten."

I reluctantly raised my head. "Yes?"

Our eyes met and held. "Don't apologize for saying what you think, for expecting better from people. I don't see Paris the way you do, but I'd like to. I came here looking for answers, but I'm beginning to wonder if I wasn't asking all the wrong questions."

I shook my head. "Stop. I know I said I wanted romance, but please don't shovel it on so thick. We've both been very clear about where this is going."

He was quiet for a moment; then a hint of a smile returned to his eyes. "Oh yes, a week of hot-and-heavy sex, temporary monogamy, lingerie, a silent vibrator, and some crepes. Romance—but no bullshit."

I unclenched my hand, laying it flat against his chest. "When you say it that way, it sounds . . ."

"Amazing." A teasing light shone in his eyes. *"Minou."*

"Don't you dare." My jaw dropped at his use of the naughty French term for *cat*. I smacked his chest and went to step back, but he held me to him. "Oh, and don't think I'm not going to google French terms for male genitalia—"

His smile sent my threat straight out of my head. He whispered into my ear, "Why google something I could teach you . . . while referring to a rather impressive example."

"I wish I could think of something snarky to say." I stroked myself across his hard-on.

His growl was guttural. "I wish I could think about anything beyond fucking you."

I'd never been a woman men fawned over. I didn't drive them wild, test their control. Whether it was true or pure fantasy, I loved the idea that Mauricio might be as affected by me as I was by him. Cecile said there was nothing better than good sex without the pressure of more.

I hadn't agreed with her.

I wasn't sure I was capable of it.

But hot damn I wanted to be with Mauricio.

Not after the tour—now.

I opened my mouth to say just that, but before I had a chance to, Mauricio stepped back and said, "I'd like a second chance at the question you asked me."

Had I asked something? Who the hell could remember? "Okay."

He turned so we were both looking down the center street of Île Saint-Louis. "When I look down this road, I see possibilities—to hear what you know about the area, to see what you'll want at that little shop, to buy ice cream for you from Berthillon, then taste it on your lips. I know a boutique nearby where we can buy that toy you want. I want to be there the first time you use it. I want to see you learn to please yourself; then I'll show you how to make it even better. Are you wet just thinking about coming for me? If we were alone, my fingers would already be inside you. My tongue would already know the taste of you." The heat of him behind me had me wanting to turn and throw myself back into his arms, but I forced myself to stay as I was. He bent next to my ear and asked, "How is that for romance with no bullshit? Is that what you're looking for?"

"It'll do," I croaked, then cleared my throat. My sex pulsed in anticipation.

He kissed my neck just below my ear. "Glad I finally got it right."

Mauricio took my hand in his, and we began to walk down the sidewalk together. The buildings were still as impressive, the cobblestone just as old, but all my attention was focused on the man beside me.

We went into the shops, and some of them might have had the trinkets I'd said I wanted to purchase for friends back home, but I didn't buy anything. I told him more about the history of Paris than he likely wanted to know, but he looked interested. We swapped college and childhood stories over paninis we ate on a bench down on the quay by the river. I don't know if I took a bite of what I ordered. The day had taken on a dreamlike quality.

And the ice cream? It made our kisses deliciously cold and sweet.

I would have followed him anywhere that day, but when we left the island I clung to his hand because I knew where we were headed. There's a difference between agreeing to have sex with a man and going shopping with him for a sex toy.

One was a rush.

The other was equal parts exciting and scary.

I tried to look casual as we walked into a small boutique with lingerie displayed in the window. Mauricio spoke to the female shopkeeper in fluent French. She answered him, then asked me something and waited for a response. I simply nodded even though I had no idea what she'd said.

Mauricio shook his head and said something in French, then murmured to me in English, "She said we're welcome to look around and asked if we'd like her to explain how any of them work. I told her you were already a knowledgeable connoisseur."

I playfully tightened my fingers around his. "I'm surprised you didn't say you're a sex toy guru and I'm your convert."

He smiled and arched his eyebrows.

I gasped and laughed. "You did. That's exactly what you said to her, isn't it?"

"I may have implied I was capable of explaining anything you needed to know." The smile he shot me melted away my mock outrage. "Did you really want her lingering with us? I didn't."

It was impossible not to smile back at him. "Fine, but if you call me 'kitten' while we're here, I will tie your balls in a sheepshank knot."

"That's a very specific threat"—he pulled at the neck of his shirt— "and a man's package is nothing to joke about breaking."

"Then don't call me a vagina, not even in French."

He blinked a few times, looked like he was holding back a laugh, and said, "Understood." He cleared his throat. "Now that we've cleared that up, why don't we check out what they have in stock?"

CHAPTER ELEVEN

MAURICIO

The layout of the store was designed to put customers at ease. I led Wren through it to a back area, where the more intimate items were displayed. Although this particular store was new to me, my first French lover had taken me to a similar one. She'd been twenty years my senior, and I'd been wide eyed . . . the way Wren was as she stood before a wall of dildos and butt plugs.

The advice I'd received long ago came back to me. I caressed Wren's back as I spoke. "The mistake people make is thinking they should like everything here. No one wants everything they see on a menu, and they don't feel strange about having a preference when it comes to ordering something to eat. This is no different. First, what is your spice level?"

She was tense beneath my touch, but she didn't look like she wanted to bolt. She pointed to a double dildo about the size of her arm. "That's too much."

I would have laughed, but she was serious. "I agree."

She picked up a box that contained a multimotored vibrator with several moving parts and read the directions in English. "This one looks complicated."

"I'm sure you could master it, but there are simpler ones."

She scanned the shelf with the diligence of someone performing a quality inspection. So adorably fascinated I couldn't look away. She picked up a whip, cracked it, then put it back down. "I think I'd punch you if you whipped me with that."

Was she deliberately testing my ability to keep a straight face? "I've never been punched during sex and can't say I want to be, so keep looking."

We made our way over the shelves of vibrators. She scanned the items, put her hands on her hips, and pursed her lips. "I didn't know there were so many kinds."

I cleared my throat. It was difficult to think with all my blood heading south, but I wanted her to leave with something she'd enjoy. "Since you said you're looking for something quiet, I'd suggest something like this." I chose an insertable vibrator that was designed to be worn beneath clothing. "The remote control is an added benefit."

She spun to face me. "And who'd be in charge of it? You?"

Two could play the ultraserious game. I made a show of looking over the box carefully before saying, "I don't see my name in the instructions. Strange. I guess that means either one of us could hold the remote." A hint of uncertainty entered her eyes, and I felt like an ass for teasing her. She'd said that back home she was one of the guys. I could see how her straightforward nature might intimidate them. Wren was an intelligent woman who wasn't afraid to say what she thought. She was also more sensitive than she first appeared. "Wren, I'm just giving you shit. I don't care if we leave with all of these toys or none of them. I'd gladly fuck you all night or leave you at your door with a kiss. If this isn't fun for both of us, we're doing something wrong."

She searched my face, then nodded slowly. "You'd really be okay with ending the day with a kiss?"

A slow anger burned through me. Had she been with someone who hadn't been? If I learned she had, I'd find the bastard and teach him what real men think of pieces of shit like that. "Always, Wren. Don't ever be with someone who isn't. Not sexually. Not even for coffee."

She placed her hand flat on my chest. My heartbeat accelerated beneath it. "You're not supposed to be a nice guy too."

I brought her hand to my lips and kissed it. "So many rules. Come out and play with me, Wren. No pressure. We'll see where this goes."

That beautiful blush of hers returned. "What happened to 'You're mine until Saturday'?" Her mimic of my voice was comical.

I wiggled my eyebrows at her. "I can be that man, too, if you like it."

Her eyes darkened with desire. "I did like it—even more now that I met this side of you. You role-play. I've always wanted to do that." Her hand slid down my stomach and cupped my throbbing cock. "I'll be disappointed if you leave me with a kiss."

"Understood," I said in a strangled voice. Holy shit. Her hand trailed its way back to my pecs, then fell away, and she simply held my gaze.

We stood there, not speaking. Not moving. So turned on I swear we could have come without touching.

The sound of the box dropping from my hand to the floor brought us back to the moment. We both bent to retrieve it and nearly knocked heads. With a laugh, I let her get it and straightened.

She looked the box over, then smiled at me. "So, my sex toy guru, what would you have your student do with this?"

I shuddered and groaned. I wanted to steal her away back to my hotel and show her, but I also didn't want to rush through the anticipation of being with her. Had I ever wanted a woman as much as I wanted her? Fuck, had there been women before her? Did they have names? Faces? They faded away as I looked into her eyes. "Let's buy it. I'm sure they'll let you have a moment in their changing room."

"You want me to use it now?" Her voice rose as she asked the question.

I lowered mine and whispered in her ear, "I want you to want to use it now. They sell batteries. This place is discreet. And we're not done with the bus tour."

"No."

"Okay," I said, but I smiled. No wasn't what I saw in her eyes.

"Okay," she said in a rush. "I'll do it. Oh my God, I can't believe I'm agreeing to this."

The shopkeeper came over. I explained the situation to her. She didn't even blink. I paid for the toy and watched as Wren headed into a changing room with a pack of batteries and our purchase.

I stood just outside the door. After what seemed like endless rustling of packaging being opened, Wren said, "Mauricio?"

"Yes?" I leaned closer to the door.

"You can't hear it, can you?"

I covered my face with a hand and gave in to a chuckle. "Not a sound."

"Once it's in, no one will be able to, right?"

"I'll warn you if I hear so much as a peep." I thought about what a novice she was and asked, "Would you like me to buy some lube?"

Her voice was deeper and husky when she answered. "No. Thank you. It's already in. And, wow. That's quite a motor it has."

I swallowed hard and took a deep, calming breath. "You can adjust it up and down to suit what you like."

"Do I just leave it on?"

"Whatever feels good." You know the pill warning that suggests calling one's doctor if experiencing a four-hour erection? I'd always found that commercial amusing, but now that I was experiencing one, I could see how it might be a problem. A man's brain does funny things when it goes without blood for an extended period of time.

When she walked out of the changing room with an excited flush on her cheeks and waving the toy remote proudly at me, I saw forever with her. The whole fucking thing . . . five kids, holidays with my family, visits with hers. I imagined her in my bed, my car, my house. Naked. Dressed. Laughing together. Crying. It shook me to the core and left me open mouthed and staring at her.

She walked right up to me and whispered, "You really can't hear it?"

My mouth moved but no words came out.

She gave me a funny look. "Are you okay? Did something happen?"

I shook my head. "I'm fine." She looked at me expectantly, and I realized I hadn't answered her question. "Nothing. Absolutely silent."

"Even now?" she asked and closed her eyes halfway. "That setting might be too good to do in public."

Only because I knew such boutiques frown on anything graphic happening inside their store, I took her by the hand and hauled her outside. Once on the sidewalk, I pulled her to me and kissed her long and deep.

When I ended the kiss, we were both breathing raggedly. I kept her tucked against me as I tried to regain control.

"I can't," she said softly, and a piece of me died.

I'd told her I was okay with whatever she wanted, and I'd meant it. But, holy fuck, it wouldn't be easy if she said no. "Can't what?"

"I can't get on a bus with strangers and children with this thing in me."

I relaxed. "Okay. So, is this you begging me to stop the tour?"

She laughed softly, causing her tits to move deliciously up and down on my chest. "I guess it is."

"I rented out a penthouse not too far from here."

She moved back and forth against me, nearly making me once again incapable of speech. She touched a button on the remote and gasped. "Yes, but on one condition . . ."

"Yes?" If she'd asked me for my fortune, I would have given it to her. My baseball card collection? It would have been hers. My signed jersey from Tom Brady? Done. Whatever.

"Can you talk dirty to me again? That was hot."

I hauled her to my side, and after I hailed a cab, I described in filthy detail every last thing I wanted to do to her. As we rode across town, I continued to whisper scenarios to her, highlighting them with my favorite techniques.

She came once in the back of the taxi. Quietly, covertly. She closed her eyes, gripped my hand, and bit her bottom lip as it washed over her. I adjusted my position to block the view of the driver. That moment, that gift, was all mine to enjoy.

When we pulled up to my hotel, I paid the driver and guided Wren to the private elevator that went only to the top floor. As the doors closed behind us, I kissed her, but I kept myself in check. What I wanted to do to her didn't belong on a security video cam.

Once the elevator doors opened into the penthouse, it was game on. I lifted her by her hips. She wrapped her legs around my waist, and I carried her across the foyer toward the bedroom. She ground her vibrating sex against me and opened her mouth wide for my tongue.

Patience expended, I tore her shirt up and over her head. Her bra hit the floor a second later. She feverishly unbuttoned my shirt and pulled it from my trousers before tossing that to the floor as well.

Her breasts were as beautiful as I imagined, large enough to bury my face between. I bent her back over my forearm and spent some quality time on each. All the while, I felt the hum of her vibrator against my stomach.

Bed or conference table?

Arm of the couch?

What was the most fucking romantic? I couldn't decide, so I lowered her right there in the foyer and stripped her naked. She just as eagerly removed the rest of my clothing.

I took a moment to appreciate the perfection of her, then donned a condom. I didn't want to rush, but the way I was feeling I also didn't want to forget. Then I started a deliberately slow exploration of her with my mouth. She was already wet and ready, but I wanted her crying for it.

I took the remote from her hand and placed it on a table before dropping to my knees before her. I placed one of her legs on my shoulder and took the toy in my hand, pulling it partially out, then sliding it back in. She gripped my shoulders with both hands and leaned back onto the wall for support.

In and out.

Back and forth until she was moaning and writhing.

I removed the toy and replaced it with my mouth, drinking in the taste of her. I flicked my tongue across her engorged clit, slowly at first, then faster and faster. I gently thrust two fingers in her wet sex and, with confidence, sought what some men never found. When I found it, she jutted her pelvis against my hand and called out my name.

Tongue. Fingers. G-spot. I could have brought her to climax then, but I selfishly wanted to join her on her next.

I brought her to the brink, then withdrew my hand and stood. As we kissed I lifted her again and drove my cock deeply into her. Nothing says "I like you" like a good wall fucking. We kissed. I didn't go easy on her, and she begged me for even more.

"Oh yes," she said over and over as I pounded into her. "Oh my God, yes."

"You like it rough, Kitten?" I growled and dug my hand into her hair.

She clenched around me. "I like everything you do. Don't stop."

"Stop? This is just the beginning."

We turned so my back was against the wall and I could raise and lower her on my cock. She dug her nails into my arms and threw her head back. I thrust harder and harder into her.

Only when her eyes began to close and I saw her giving herself over to an orgasm did I let myself go. Wildly, roughly, I turned and pounded into her until I joined her with a mind-erasing fucking explosion of an orgasm.

We stayed there, leaning against the wall, still connected for several minutes. Eventually I lowered her slowly to her feet and cleaned myself off. We might have ended there, but I'd made promises, and I intended to keep all of them.

It was the honorable thing to do.

I rinsed off her toy and handed it back to her, this time picking up the remote for myself. "Put it back in, Kitten; then I want you down on your knees."

Her face was beautiful flushed. Her hair mussed and lips plump from my kiss. My cock twitched back to full mast in anticipation.

She handed me back the toy. "You want me on my knees, you put it back in."

I could love this woman.

"Yes, ma'am," I said in a duly serious tone. Then for flair, I put both the toy and the remote in one hand and bent to swing her over my shoulder.

She laughed and flailed. Her breasts bounced on my back. I carried her to the bedroom and tossed her on the bed.

Eyes dark with desire, she pulled her knees up and spread her legs for me. I inserted the vibrator gently and turned it on, moving it back and forth until she made a sound that said it was sitting just right.

I moved to the side of the bed with the remote still in my hand. "Come here, Kitten." When she didn't immediately move, I raised the level of vibration.

She rolled up and onto her knees and crawled over to the edge of the bed. "Yes, my guru?"

"Take me into your mouth, Wren. Take me so deep. I want to fuck your mouth."

She did. As her lips and tongue worked their magic, I raised the level of her pleasure. Soon we were moaning together. She was a natural at knowing just what to do with her hands. Her lips closed tight around me. Her tongue teased and circled. She worked my balls like a pro.

I raised the vibration even more and loved how she paused to savor the sensation.

When I came she swallowed, and I named our first child.

I changed my mind later about *Holy Fuck Romano*, but in that moment it sounded good.

Everything was good.

I laid her back on the bed and loved her until she had her own explosion; then I cuddled her to my side and pulled a blanket over both of us. This was normally when I'd be coming back to earth and hoping the woman knew to leave rather than stay. I tightened my hold on Wren and fought sleep. Her eyes were already closed.

I wanted to wake to her.

There was so much more I wanted to do.

So much more I wanted to learn. What had she liked most? What did she want more of?

For the first time in my life, I didn't want to wake alone. I wanted to make this woman crepes, all the goddamned crepes she could eat. And then spend the rest of the night burning those calories off.

CHAPTER TWELVE

WREN

Tucked against Mauricio's side, eyes shut, I fought a wave of panic. If he hadn't been holding me, I probably would have already been dressed and out the door.

Sex with a stranger was not supposed to be that good.

It shouldn't have felt so right.

I didn't even know his last name.

Five days, that was all he'd promised. Fun sex.

I shouldn't love the scent of him. I couldn't let myself relax into his embrace because no matter how good it felt, none of this was real. No wonder he walked around like he was God's gift to women . . .

I took a moment to thank the man upstairs for this experience. Now, some might think it was wrong to send up a thank-you for what might be considered immoral . . . but I'd just been shown how good sex was supposed to be, and that wasn't something I took lightly.

Had I married any of my past lovers, I would have been sentencing myself to a lifetime of mediocre. I had no idea this was possible.

Sure, I'd heard it could be, but I didn't really believe it. I thought it was like when everyone in church said they were praying but they were really daydreaming. Maybe some of them were really praying.

Who knew?

Mauricio's eyes were closed, and his breathing had deepened, so I attempted to slip out of his embrace. His arms tightened around me. "Stay," he murmured.

Was he even awake? Maybe he said that to every woman he took to his bed.

It felt way too good to be in his arms, in his bed.

I started to hyperventilate. Space. I needed to put some space between us so I could wrap my head around what had just happened.

This was only tragic if I made it tragic.

Only a bad idea if I did something stupid like start to have feelings for him.

I tried to slip away again. He buried his face in my hair and inhaled. "You smell so damn good."

When my phone rang, I bolted for it, breaking free. "I should get that."

Mauricio rolled over onto his side and propped up on one elbow, watching me.

Buck naked, I sat cross-legged on the carpeted floor and answered my phone.

"How was your date?" Cecile asked. "Want to get something to eat together? I have so much to tell you."

"I had a nice day." I met Mauricio's gaze and mouthed, "Cecile." He nodded.

"Why do you sound so weird?" Cecile asked.

"No reason."

"Are you still with him?"

"Yes."

"You have to tell me . . . did you actually go on the bus tour?" she asked with a laugh.

I couldn't decipher the expression on Mauricio's face. He looked as confused as I felt. No, that had to be wrong. He was the one who did this all the time. "We took the tour. Now we're just . . . hanging out."

He arched an eyebrow, and amusement filled his eyes.

"You fucked him," Cecile exclaimed. "Was it good?"

"Can we discuss this later?" Had Mauricio heard her? His grin said he might have.

"Because he's still there. I get it. Fine. I can wait. But listen, I held up my side of the deal. I met Felix's parents, and you are not going to believe what I learned."

I leaned forward and for a second forgot about my audience. "What? What did they say?"

"He wasn't with another woman. He was injured at work. It was serious enough to require surgery. He didn't want me to know because he was embarrassed. I guess he thinks I won't see him the same way, but accidents happen to everyone."

"Injured? What happened?"

"They didn't give me too many details, but the recovery will take weeks."

"Is he still in the hospital?"

"No, he's recuperating at his apartment. I want to drop by with some food for him or something. What do you think? We're not on a take-care-of-each-other-when-we're-sick level, but I care about him as a person. I'd bring food to any friend who was injured."

I chewed my bottom lip and met Mauricio's gaze again. He was definitely listening in. "Cecile is thinking about dropping by to see Felix. Maybe bring him some soup or something. What do you think?"

He sat straight up. "Bad idea. No."

I frowned at him. "It wouldn't be to stay. She just wants to show him that she cares."

"I guarantee you he does not want her there."

Mauricio was adamant, and my chest tightened with emotion. I was offended *for* Cecile. It was also a smack of reality for me. *You know what? Fuck Felix. Fuck you too, Mauricio.* "Mauricio thinks you should go. I do too. Don't even call. Just drop by with something. If he's not a complete douche, he'll be glad you did."

With narrowed eyes, I silently dared Mauricio to say differently.

He rubbed both hands over his face and groaned.

"You really think so?" Cecile asked.

"I do," I assured her. The best cure for confusion was to take a good long look at the truth, no matter how ugly it was. If Felix turned Cecile away, her feelings might be hurt, but she would see that being with a man who didn't care about her was a waste of her time.

Even if the sex was good.

"Okay. I will. I'll call you later and tell you how it goes."

"Cecile, do me a favor . . ."

"What?"

"If he isn't nice about your visit, give him hell for it."

"Oh, you don't have to worry about me, Wren. I can take care of myself."

"I know. Just don't accept less than you deserve."

"I won't."

After I ended the call, I placed the phone on the carpet beside me. Mauricio glanced at his phone, then back at me. How was it possible that after one day I could almost hear his thoughts? "You want to call Felix to warn him."

"He's been a good friend to me," Mauricio said with an apologetic grimace.

"Was he really hurt? Is he truly recovering from surgery?"

"Yes."

I threw my hands up in the air. "Then what's the big deal? They've been having sex for years. Doesn't that at least make them friends?"

"It should."

"In my world it would make them more than that." I folded my arms across my chest and realized I was still naked when my breasts bounced beneath them. I looked around and saw nothing to cover myself with, so I stood and went to the nearest closet. The T-shirt I chose was far too big for me, but that meant it covered everything I wanted it to. Hands on my hips, I stood beside the bed and looked down at the man who had just given me a few hours I'd never forget. "I can't do this. I don't want to do this. I won't be Cecile."

He scooted across the bed and rose to stand in front of me. When he reached for me, I stepped back and he dropped his hands. "You're not Cecile, and I'm not Felix."

I took a step back. "This was great. Phenomenal even, but—"

He took a step to close the distance between us. "Stay, Kitten."

I retreated a few feet. "See, that's the thing. I'm not really a sex kitten. This isn't my scene, and you're not my type."

Okay, honestly, the Adonis that stood before me in full naked glory was every woman's type, but I meant on a deeper level.

A frown creased his forehead. "And what is your type?"

"You're beautiful, but I need more. I want someone I have things in common with. Someone who gets my jokes even if I leave the punch line off." I retreated another few feet. "I want something real."

"Wren, if I did something—"

I turned and fled to the foyer, where all my clothes were. He followed, dick waving as he approached. I threw his pants at him. "Could you put something on, please?"

He stepped into them.

I found my underwear and donned them, then put my jeans on. Without speaking I shimmied my bra on beneath his oversize T-shirt.

Bare chested—beautifully, deliciously bare chested—he stood beside me as I stepped into my shoes. The sadness in his eyes made me feel guilty about the way I was leaving. He'd been nothing but good to me . . . and I mean *good*.

How could I explain that was part of the problem? If things hadn't been so perfect, maybe, maybe we could have had until Saturday. I couldn't risk the kind of hurt I saw looming if I let this go too far. "I'm sorry," I said gruffly. "You didn't do anything wrong. You did everything right, too right, which is why I have to leave. I know that sounds fucked up, but it's how I feel. I don't regret today. I just—" I remembered my vibrator. "Should I leave it? Take it? See, that's my point. I don't know. But more than that, I don't think I want to know. I don't want to be a person who fucks a guy, grabs her new vibrator, and goes home like nothing happened."

"Good," he said in a husky tone, "because both your vibrator and I want you to stay."

I blinked back tears. "You don't have to pretend you do. See, that's the thing. I thought I wanted the fantasy, but I don't think I do want to be swept off my feet. I'm sorry."

He walked with me to the door. "I don't know what you want me to say, Wren. I don't want you to leave. I don't have more than that."

A heaviness settled in my heart. "And you shouldn't, because we don't really know each other. That's the point, right? You asked me to come out and play and I did. Now I just want to go home."

"Home? You're leaving Paris?"

He was such a good actor. Honestly, I almost believed he cared if we never saw each other again. I shook my head. "Not yet. I meant my rental. Thank you for today, Mauricio."

I went to open the elevator door.

He placed his hand over the call button. "Wait. You can't leave like this."

I met his gaze. "You're the one who said I should never be with someone who didn't respect what I want. I want to go home, Mauricio. Let me go."

He dropped his hand. "Do you want me to call you a car?"

I shook my head. "I can catch a taxi on my own."

He looked about to say something more, but I pressed the call button, ducked into the elevator, and left before he had a chance to. On the ride down I realized I was still wearing his shirt.

I half expected him to meet me when the elevator doors opened, but he didn't. He didn't race to the street to ask me to stay. Didn't text me not to go.

I didn't want him to.

But I was disappointed that he hadn't.

It was still light out when I arrived back at my apartment. I locked the door behind me, threw the key on the counter, and took a long, hot shower. And all the while I told myself I'd made the right choice to leave.

I thought it as I snacked on a stale baguette.

I thought it again as I flipped through endless channels in French before I found a news station in English.

It was practically a mantra by the time I flopped down on my bed and stared at the ceiling as the sun finally set. I turned off the lights, then checked if Mauricio had texted.

And told myself I was happy he hadn't.

Each time I tossed and turned, I reminded myself that being alone was better than being with someone who didn't care about me.

Just before I fell asleep, I wondered if he was anywhere near as confused as I was.

CHAPTER THIRTEEN

MAURICIO

I swore under my breath as I paced from room to room in my empty penthouse. Simply because I didn't want the maid to have to do it, I rinsed off Wren's toy and put it in my luggage. It sat on a pile of my socks like a modern-day Cinderella slipper left at the ball.

Which made me what? The Prince of Dumbasses? I could have told her why Felix didn't want company. I should have.

But it wasn't my story to tell.

I didn't call Felix to warn him about Cecile's impending visit, though. Partly because it wasn't smart to get involved in anything as tangled as that, but mostly because I agreed with Wren. After years of sleeping with Cecile, Felix should have the balls to tell her why he didn't want to see her.

If he still had balls. Maybe they dry up and fall off when a man breaks his dick. I didn't know, and I hoped I'd never find out.

I shook my head to dispel the image of Felix with raisins for 'nads.

My phone was still on my bed. I picked it up and typed: I'm sorry, Kitten.

No, that wasn't right. She didn't like that nickname. Because she liked it too much? I'd done everything right and somehow done it all wrong.

How the fuck does that happen?

And what am I sorry about?

I'm not sorry.

I deleted the message.

You're impossible to please.

It was true. She wanted romance, but not just any romance. She wanted the version she had in her head, and I was supposed to be a mind reader.

How could I get a joke if she left the punch line off? Who is capable of that?

I'd been honest with her at every point. I would have sat on that fucking bus with her all day and put a damn ice pack on my raging hard-on if she'd wanted to take it slowly.

But no . . . she wanted a toy.

And she wanted everything buying one led to.

Three orgasms. Some women are happy with one. Three. And she still stormed off.

I can't believe I wanted to make breakfast for her.

That probably would have been too much for her too.

Oh, no, you made my coffee just the way I like it. What an asshole.

I deleted the message and was in the process of writing another one I didn't intend to send when my phone rang. Was it her?

No.

"Hi, Dad."

"Sebastian said you were thinking about coming back early. Did you ever hear from Felix?"

I sat on the edge of my bed. "I did. He was hurt at work, and that was why he missed our meeting."

"I hope he's okay."

"He's fine." Unless he'd said something stupid to Cecile and she strangled him. "Just one of those embarrassing injuries no one wants to talk about. So don't mention it to anyone."

"I won't. How is Paris? Is it as good as you remember?"

My father's voice always calmed me. He was as easygoing as he was big hearted. Nothing ever made him angry, and no one had ever disappointed him to the point where they weren't welcome in his home. No exaggeration, I'd won the lottery with parents. My mother was his stricter-but-just-as-loving counterpart. Together they had taught my brothers and me that family was the foundation a person built their life on. Nothing else mattered as much.

The money we'd made? Mention it and my father would scoff and say he had one store back when he lived in Italy, and he was happy.

My brothers and I argued when we were younger, even came to blows at times—we were four boys in one house. But my father never let us end the day angry with each other. When we fought, he assigned us chores we had to do together. None of us were done until all of us were. Side by side. We worked as one unit, the way a family was meant to. And it worked. It taught us to pull together when things went south.

That philosophy had guided us through the dark days after Sebastian's first wife had died. Something like that might have torn another family apart, but we were each other's strength. So we stayed by Sebastian even when he told us to leave. We forgave him, cheered him on, gave him room to fail when he needed to.

I told my father the truth, because the Romano family valued honesty. "It's different, Dad. I'm not the person I was when I lived here."

"You were a boy back then. All you wanted was fun. You're a man now. Of course you want something different."

"Yeah. That's what I'm struggling with. I don't know what I want. I enjoy working for Romano Superstores, but it's not a passion for me."

"A passion. Okay. Is this where you tell me you want to be on stage in tights spinning around?"

I laughed, which had been his intention. I got my sense of humor from him. Also my good nature. If there was someone who didn't like him, I'd never met them. "Not exactly. Tutus have never looked good on me. They make me look fat."

He chuckled. "So, are you coming home?"

"Not yet. Dad, I have a serious question for you."

"Oh, a serious one. Let me sit down. Shoot."

"When you met Mom, did you know right away she was the one for you, or did you go through a period of believing you were losing your mind first?"

"You met someone."

"Yes. No. Maybe. I don't know. I may never see her again. We had one date, and I messed it up royally. Or I did such a great job that I spooked her. I'm not saying I love her. I don't even know her last name. All I'm saying is this might be the one."

My father did what I should have guessed he'd do . . . he called my mother over. "Mauricio finally met a woman."

He said it like I'd never landed a woman in my life.

Worse, my mother's excitement soared. "Put him on speakerphone."

"Hi, Mom."

"Mauricio, is it true? Did you meet someone? What's her name?"

"Easy, Mom. I probably won't even see her again."

Dad chimed in. "He asked if I knew right away that you were the one."

"He did?" My mother's voice rose happily. "I'm so happy for you, Mauricio. First, Sebastian. Now you. Our house will soon be full of grandchildren."

Mentioning Wren might have been a bad idea.

"I'd hold off on planning the wedding. Our first date didn't end on a good note."

Mom huffed, "Then you go see her tomorrow morning and fix things."

Fix things? "I have an alternate plan. Could we forget I brought her up?"

"I knew the first time I saw her, Mauricio," Dad said. "No other woman mattered after I laid eyes on her. She didn't make it easy. Gave me a real run for my money, but I didn't doubt we'd be together because . . ."

I leaned forward with my phone. "Because?"

He cleared his throat. "Because the first time she kissed me, I saw our future together—everything. I don't believe in psychics or things like that, so I can't explain it. All I know is I could see her by my side . . . always. Making it happen took time, but everything I saw that day came to be."

I saw that too—with Wren. My heart started thudding wildly in my chest. *I saw everything we could be, everything I wanted us to be.*

It was craziness.

Mom interjected, "Your father was relentless. Flowers every day. Presents for my family. He wouldn't take no for an answer. Then one day I couldn't remember why I'd ever said no at all, and we married."

"And?" Dad prodded.

Mom laughed. "And have been blissfully happy ever since."

"See, son, that's how it's done."

I made a face. "They have all these laws now, Dad. It's a fine line between pursuing and stalking. A flower every day? You don't think that was a bit much?" Love didn't work the way they described. That was the stuff of books. Real love was . . .

I stopped there because however it had started, my parents had a solid, loving marriage. Was it possible I was capable of that kind of devotion to someone? Before Wren, I hadn't thought so. The truth was, though, that I wanted the future I'd gotten a glimpse of, and I wanted it with Wren.

"Go big or go home," my mother said. "One of the presents he gave my father was a cow. I took offense to that. We were not in some third world country where I could be traded for livestock."

Dad chuckled. "They were farmers, and the cow was one he'd had his eye on for a while. I was shooting for practical but thoughtful."

"Whatever," Mom said, dismissing the statement with amusement. "So what about this woman? If you really are interested in her, what are you going to do about it?"

Go big or go home.

I could go big.

Like knock-her-socks-off, "holy shit this is the Paris people don't even know is possible" big. "I could plan a better date than the one we had today, something I know she'll really like."

"That's my boy," Mom said. "Call us if you need any more advice."

"No, I think I've got this," I said.

After a moment, my father lowered his voice and asked, "Did you kiss her yet?"

"Yes, Dad."

"How many did you see?"

"How many what?"

"Children."

Ridiculous.

Impossible.

Completely insane.

"Five. I saw five." But that had only been because she'd said that was how many she wanted.

Right?

Dad let out a happy sigh. "Your mother is going to love this woman."

"Okay, Dad. I have to go." I cleared my throat. "And don't build this up for Mom. I like this woman, but it might go nowhere."

"We'll see, won't we?" he asked a little smugly.

"Good night, Dad."

"Love you, son."

"Love you too."

CHAPTER FOURTEEN

WREN

The next morning I was woken by Cecile texting me that she was downstairs. I buzzed her in, left the door open, and crawled back into bed. She joined me, flopping down on the other side.

I didn't need her to say a thing; I knew she was hurting. "I'm sorry, Cecile."

She gripped her hands on her stomach and looked up at the ceiling. After letting out a shaky breath, she blinked back tears. "I thought I was okay with how casual things have always been with Felix. We were never exclusive, and I was fine with it. But I thought we cared about each other."

I reached over and took one of her hands in mine, giving it a supportive squeeze.

She angrily wiped a tear away. "How could I have been so wrong about him? You know what he did when he saw me? He told me to leave and slammed the door in my face. Like I was no one to him."

Tears started filling my eyes. I sniffed loudly. I felt awful that I'd sent her into that situation. Worse, I'd done it out of a selfish desire to prove something to myself. "I shouldn't have suggested that you go there, Cecile. Mauricio thought it was a bad—"

"I know. I heard him."

"I'm so sorry, Cecile."

She shook her head. "You did me a favor, Wren. I was wasting my time with him, settling for less because it was easy. Oh my God, I wanted to punch him in the dick."

I laughed and sniffed again. "Let karma do it instead. Maybe he'll get it caught in a zipper."

She chuckled. "Or slammed in a car door."

"Ouch. How would that even happen?"

"I don't know. I just remember closing a car door on one of my fingers by accident. That's what I'd like him to experience."

Because it seemed to be cheering her, I added, "I've heard a dick can be broken. Maybe his will snap right off the next time he fucks someone."

She laughed. "Is it wrong to hope it does?"

I thought about it. "I don't think so. It means you're human. I really am sorry, Cecile. I wish he'd been the man you thought he was."

She let out an audible breath. "Me too." She gave my hand a squeeze before releasing it. "So, enough of that. Tell me about your date with Mauricio. I'm impressed that you got him to go on the tour."

I turned onto my side, tucking a hand under my head. "You were right about him. He wanted to leave after the first stop. I'm glad you're here, because I've been thinking in circles all night." She mirrored my position, and it felt so much like we were back in college my eyes teared up again.

Her expression darkened. "If he hurt you, I'll kill him."

"He didn't." I blinked away my tears. "Sorry, it's just so good to see you again."

She nodded, then waved a hand at me. "Stop, you're going to make me cry, and I'm not sentimental. And cough up the details."

I told her about how he'd almost left until I'd said what it meant if he did and how he'd sworn he'd ride the bus all day if I wanted.

"I like that," she said.

"I did too." I told her about visiting Île Saint-Louis and how confused I'd been there—how I'd wanted him to be as into history as I was.

"I couldn't care less about history and we get on," she said.

I frowned. "I thought you didn't like Mauricio."

"I never said that. I told you he's not *your* type. I warned you to be careful. I just don't think two people have to be clones of each other to be compatible."

I could see that. "The rest of the day was pretty incredible." I told her about how easy he was to talk to, how much we laughed together. When I got to the point where we were at the adult toy store, she raised a hand.

"Whoa. Whoa. Whoa. You went sex toy shopping with him? You? Whose idea was that?"

I smiled proudly. "Mine. Well, buying the toy was all me. He chose the store."

"So . . ."

"It was a lot of fun. And everything that followed was great. Mind-blowing. Life-changing good."

Her eyes narrowed. "But?"

I started to speak, then stopped. I didn't want to say anything that would add to how sad she already was.

She knew me too well. "You think he's like Felix."

I wrinkled my nose. "Don't you?"

She sighed. "I don't know. They're friends. From what I've heard, they ran with a pretty wild crowd a few years back. Felix adores him. Today, that's not such a good character reference."

"You told me he would sell me a fantasy and then forget me when he was done. I had no idea how easy it could be to forget it's not real. He says everything I want to hear. There were times yesterday when I felt a real connection. And the sex . . . it won't be easy to be with someone else after him. It was that good."

"So what do you want to do?"

"I told him I didn't want the fantasy he was feeding me. And then I left. I was pretty blunt. Considering he hasn't texted or anything, I'd say what I want is a moot point. It's over."

"That's a pretty passive approach to life."

I tilted my head in confusion. "It's called being realistic."

She made a face.

I sat up. "Say it."

She shrugged one shoulder. "Nothing. Just, now I understand how you've stayed for so long in a job you hate."

"One has nothing to do with the other."

"They're both examples of you holding back because you're afraid to lose."

"Sorry if I'm cautious; you just had a door slammed in your face by a man you slept with for years." As soon as the words came out of my mouth, I regretted them. "I'm sorry. That was low. I don't know why I said it."

Cecile sat up and looked me in the eye. "It's okay. No one likes to hear the truth. Not me. Not *you*."

I shook my head slowly. "I'm not as strong as you, Cecile. I might fall for this guy. Being with him was like nothing I've experienced before. I'm scared."

"We're all scared, Wren. Just because we're adults doesn't mean we have anything figured out. I'm not in love with Felix. He's not the best sex I've ever had. He's been a reliable, good time—but mind-blowing? No. If I felt half as much for a guy as you've described it was like with Mauricio, I'd at least go back for a second helping."

"Even if there's a good chance he'll break my heart?"

She moved to the edge of the bed and stood. "A couple of days ago I would have said no. In fact, I did say Mauricio was a bad idea. But I've just been emotionally bitch-slapped by mediocrity, and I've changed my mind. From now on, I refuse to waste a single moment with a man who doesn't blow my mind. I'm done with good enough. I want fuck-ing incredible."

I moved to stand as well. "You deserve incredible."

She hugged me. "So do you, Wren." She gathered up her purse. "For what it's worth, my gut says Mauricio will call you today. Especially if it was as good for him as it was for you."

With a shrug, I joked, "Engineers are great in bed. We know how things work."

She laughed; then her expression sobered. "I know I asked you to come to Paris, but I want to head back to London—in fact my plane is readied and waiting for me. You can come with me if you want."

I thought it over. "I'm going to stay. There is still a lot I want to see. I understand why you want to leave, and it's okay. I don't need a babysitter, and I love Paris."

She gave me another hug. "I miss you already."

I squeezed her in return. "I feel the same." Then I stepped back. "Now get out of here. I have a whole city to explore."

She nodded. "Call me if you need me. I can be here in a couple hours, and my flat has a spare room if you change your mind."

"I'm fine." I walked her to the door, then leaned against it after closing it behind her. She'd given me a lot to think about.

Was it fear that held me at my job? I'd thought I'd stayed out of duty—because I was responsible. I thought about the riskier, potentially more exciting opportunities I'd had over the years. Had any one of them worked out, I would have still been able to help my parents while doing something more challenging.

I was afraid to spend time with Mauricio because I was afraid he might break my heart.

So that safe husband I was planning for myself . . . would I be as unhappy with him as I was with my job? What if there wasn't another person who could make me feel the way Mauricio did?

Shouldn't I at least give incredible a chance?

I kept my phone with me while I dressed and put on makeup. After the way I'd left, he might have already written me off.

I met my eyes in the mirror and imagined how the conversation would go if I called him. "Hi, Mauricio. Remember when I said I didn't want to be a sex kitten? And that I wanted more than I could find with you? I kind of had that backward. What I meant to say was . . . I totally enjoyed everything we did and would love to belong to you until Saturday."

There had to be a better way.

I picked up my phone and stared at it.

I'm not passive. I'm just going to call him and ask him to lunch.

My hand shook, and I took a fortifying breath.

Or I could text him something sexy. I can do sexy. Let's see.

I typed: How are you and my vibrator doing today?

No, that's stupid. And weird.

I was about to delete it when my phone rang. Mauricio.

I hit the screen to accept it and must have hit it twice because I not only answered but also sent him my text. *Shit.*

"Morning, Wren."

I missed "Kitten." *I have problems.* "Morning."

"I know how we ended things last night, but I'd love to take you out tonight. I have a couple surprises planned I think you'll really like." I heard his phone cut out. *Please don't be my text arriving.* "Did you just send me a text?"

I wanted to claim I hadn't. If I could have thought of one possible scenario in which a complete stranger might have sent him that specific message via my number, I would have run with it. Unfortunately, all I was left with was: "You don't have to read it now."

His laugh said my suggestion had come too late. "We're both fine, thank you."

I groaned. "I didn't mean to send that to you."

"Who did you mean to send it to?" He laughed.

"Of course I wrote it for you. It's not like I ran around Paris last night buying toys and sleeping with other men." I stopped talking because I wasn't making the situation better.

After an awkward silence, he asked, "Wren?"

"Yes."

"Don't worry. I wrote at least two messages to you last night that I'm glad I didn't send."

I smiled. "Really?"

"Really."

"What were they?"

"Oh. Um. I can't remember."

"Liar."

"Possibly. Or I wisely deleted them from not only my phone but my memory as well."

"Tell me one. Just one."

My phone beeped with a message. I'm sorry, Kitten.

I smiled again. *Kitten.* "You don't have to be sorry. You didn't do anything wrong."

"That's why I didn't send it."

Hmm. Now I needed to know the other. "What was the other message?"

"You asked for one, and I gave you one."

"Now I'm asking for the other."

"A lot of people would be satisfied with the apology."

"I'm not *a lot of people*. And I'm curious."

"I'm not telling you the second one."

"Why not?"

"Nothing good would come from it."

"That's not true. I would know that you care about what I want."

"No, that wouldn't be your response."

"Try me."

My phone beeped again. You're impossible to please.

109

I gasped. "Is that what you almost wrote last night or what you think right now?"

"Last night. But it's pretty fitting right now."

"It's far from a compliment."

"I didn't say it was nice. I said nothing good would come from me sharing it. You said it would make you happy. Are you happy?"

I paced my small apartment. I wanted to say I wasn't, but it would have proven him right. Between gritted teeth I said, "Yes. I'm glad you told me the truth."

"Then we're good."

"Yes."

We shared another awkward silence that made me wonder if the connection I'd felt the day before had been in my imagination. Then he said, "My intention was to make you feel better about texting your vibrator."

My mouth twitched with humor. "I wasn't texting the toy."

"No need to be embarrassed. It missed you too. Should I get it? Put it on the phone? Give the two of you a moment?"

"You're a real ass, you know that?"

"But you're smiling, aren't you?"

"I am."

"So say yes to tonight. I don't want to brag, but I had to call in some pretty big favors to set up what I have planned. I don't usually try this hard to impress a woman."

"Because they all fall at your feet?"

"Higher, Kitten. What is your obsession with feet?"

I laughed out loud. "You really planned something special for tonight?"

"Mind-blowing special."

My thought went only one place when he said that. What I couldn't figure out was why he'd need to call in a favor with anyone to surprise me with a repeat performance of the day before. "Is this a clothing-optional surprise?"

"I like how you think, but we should keep our clothing on for what I've planned for the start of the evening. Later, when we're alone, you can feel free to be as naked as you like. I actually prefer you that way."

Warmth spread through me, but I didn't give in to it. "How should I dress then?"

"Did you buy those crazy-small underwear yet? I'd start there."

I rolled my eyes skyward even as my body flushed at the memory of his tongue flicking across my clit. "Formal. Informal. Should I wear a dress?"

"Normally, I love a good dress, but for this, jeans would be more appropriate."

"Now I'm intrigued. What do you have planned?"

"You'll have to come out to play to see."

Come out to play. I'd never hear those words again without associating them with Mauricio and how it felt to be taken by him. Saying yes to a second date almost definitely meant saying yes to more of everything we'd done the day before.

Oh yes.

"Do you need my address?"

After a moment, he purred, "We should meet there. I have a feeling if I come to your apartment, we'll head straight for your bed."

My sex clenched in anticipation. My nipples shot right to attention. He had a point. "Where and what time?"

"I'm sorry, was that a yes?"

"Obviously."

"Say it then."

"What?"

"Yes."

He chuckled. "Try it again."

"Yes," I said a little impatiently.

111

"I don't want to judge, but I believe what I have planned for tonight is worthy of a little more enthusiasm than that."

How could I not laugh at that? I did, however, think of the perfect response. I lowered my voice and did my best to mimic how I'd sounded as we'd fucked against the wall. "Yes. Oh yes. God, yes."

After a brief pause, and in a deeper voice, he said, "That works."

There was a real excitement to knowing I could turn him on the way he did me. "I thought it might."

"In fact, from now on you should answer all of my questions in that manner."

Flirting with him felt natural. In a husky tone, I said, "I'll answer all the right ones that way."

He groaned. "I've changed my mind. Let's do breakfast."

I could have said yes. I wanted to, but I liked the idea that he'd planned a date for us. I didn't want to take away from that. "Bye, Mauricio. Text me the info for tonight."

"We could have crepes . . ."

I chuckled. "Bye." I ended the call smiling.

CHAPTER FIFTEEN

MAURICIO

At shortly after eight, I stood outside a side entrance of the Louvre. Private tours were not unusual, but it had taken calling a friend who owned a real estate company to get the kind of access I wanted. He knew someone who had made the necessary contacts while organizing a similar experience for promotional purposes.

Wren was going to lose her shit when she saw what I'd scored for us.

Everything else fell away as unimportant when Wren stepped out of a taxi and looked around. I waved to her. In dark-blue jeans and a blouse, she walked toward me, and I savored every moment of the view.

She looked happy to see me, but uncertain. *Oh, does Kitten not handle the unknown well? Well, she'd better hang on for the ride, because this is only part one of what I landed for the evening.*

She stopped right before me and tilted her head back as if expecting my kiss. I offered her my arm instead. That would come later. After significant reflection, I'd concluded that the mistake I'd made the day before was rushing us. Yes, she'd suggested something that once we'd purchased had made it impossible for me to think of anything but having her, but if there was any chance that we were headed somewhere more permanent—I wanted to do this right.

Looking confused, she took my arm. I guided her past the security at the door. She looked around the museum in wonder. "You got us after-hours access?"

"I did." I could feel smugness leaking into my smile.

"Oh my God. I was planning to come here later in the week. This is so exciting. Could we start with the Egyptian collection? It has everything from ancient Egypt to the Roman and Byzantine periods. One of the world's largest collections of ancient artifacts. Thank you so much. I'm so excited I'm shaking. Some people come to the Louvre and only want to see one thing—*Mona Lisa*. It's a nice painting, but it wasn't famous until it was stolen in 1911. That's what made her globally known. I appreciate her as I appreciate any of the works by Leonardo da Vinci, but I'm more taken with the skill and precision that went into the statue of the seated scribe . . . the one with the papyrus."

We stopped when I saw two men in tuxes standing outside a closed door. "So spending some time with the *Mona Lisa* wouldn't be like a dream come true for you?"

She looked around the hallway, her attention still torn between me and the wonder of the Louvre. "I'd like to see her, of course. I guess it would be interesting for a minute. Why?"

One of the men opened the door. A woman stepped forward and held out a tray with two flutes of champagne. I handed one to Wren and downed mine in one gulp before replacing it on the tray. "That's disappointing, because time with *Mona Lisa* is all I scheduled for here."

We stepped into the almost empty room together. Two chairs were set up in front of the glass-enclosed painting. There was no other artwork in the room.

"Oh," Wren said, then sipped her champagne. "So, no full-access tour?"

"Nope, just this." I led her in front of the painting.

She looked it over. "It's beautiful." She sipped her champagne again. Without missing a beat, she impressed me again. "Did you know da Vinci used a sfumato technique to color and shade her smile? That's why if you stand at a distance and look at her eyes, it seems like she's smiling. But if you stand closer and look at her mouth, the smile disappears.

Some people say it's proof of da Vinci's level of mastery. Others argue it was less intentional."

"I didn't know that," I said, impressed with Wren's insight on a broad range of topics. "Want to see how true that is?" Together we leaned closer and looked *Mona Lisa* in the eye. "Okay, now what?" We moved back several feet together. Damned if she didn't seem to suddenly be smiling. "Wow. That's really interesting."

Wren raised and lowered her shoulders. "I thought so when I read about it."

We stood there a moment longer, simply looking at the picture. Finally, I turned and referenced the chairs behind us. "Should we—?"

"Of course."

Wren sat in one chair. I sat across from her.

She smiled at me. "This is so nice. Really. I'm sure it wasn't easy to arrange all this."

I made a sound deep in my chest. It hadn't been. "I thought it would be a nice kickoff to our night together. I have somewhere better planned for next."

She leaned in and took my hand in hers. "This is great."

A staff member came by, took our champagne glasses, and offered us some wine. We each accepted a glass. After she left, Wren and I sat back in our chairs and looked at the famous painting.

It wasn't the experience I'd imagined. "So, we have the room for an hour."

"An hour," she said, and I thought I heard humor in her voice.

With anyone else I would have been irritated, but it felt more like we were sharing a joke. "Yep. We get to sit right here with those security guards watching every move we make for"—I checked my watch—"forty-five more minutes."

She laughed—the kind of laugh a person makes when there is a librarian hovering nearby telling everyone to be quiet. "Forty-five minutes. I wish I knew something else about her."

I struck a pose, elbow on knee, an open hand splayed in the direction of the painting. "Lucky for you, I have studied her history and secrets extensively." I cleared my throat. "And by that I mean I googled her today."

Wren was a beautiful woman, even more so when she smiled. I loved how I could bring out that side of her. "Then once again, I am the student and you are the master."

Completely unfair. Her reference to the day before scrambled my thoughts and filled my head with images of her in my arms, the memory of how every inch of her tasted, how good her mouth had felt wrapped around my—

"What were we talking about?"

She swatted my arm. "You were going to teach me something."

"Right." There were things I wanted to teach her, but they would have to wait until we were alone. This was about showing her I could care about history. I began to list what I'd uncovered from doing a search on the secrets of *Mona Lisa*. Infrared had been used to uncover changes da Vinci had made, damage that had been repaired after the painting had been hit with a stone, even a possible stray eyebrow hair. Bam.

When I finished, she was giving me an odd look. I've always been good at recalling what I'd read, so I was reasonably certain it wasn't because I'd gotten some of it wrong.

I waited.

Wren looked from me to the painting and back. "You put a lot of thought into tonight."

I dipped my head in recognition.

"Thank you," she said with such sincerity it knocked me off-center for a moment.

Our eyes met and held. The sizzle from the day before was there, but there was more. I couldn't label it or explain it. It simply was. "You're welcome."

After another long pause, I looked down at my watch and proclaimed, "Only forty minutes left."

"Seriously?"

"I'm joking. Thirty." I took her hand in mine and laced my fingers through hers. "We don't have to stay."

She lightly squeezed my hand. "I want to. Seriously, Mauricio, this was incredibly thoughtful. Much more than I expected."

I raised her hand to my lips. "And the night has just begun."

CHAPTER SIXTEEN

WREN

If life had a "Rewind" button, I wouldn't have said anything I had when I'd arrived at the Louvre, but somehow it hadn't ruined the night. I wouldn't have blamed Mauricio if he'd called me ungrateful. I hadn't meant to be. Sometimes I had trouble downshifting from how I thought something would go.

Once I understood what we were doing at the Louvre and saw how he'd taken the time to actually learn about the history of the painting—for me—I loved every minute of it.

A private car had been there waiting for us as we left the museum. I'd expected Mauricio to pull me into his arms as soon as the door to it closed, but instead he held my hand and looked excited about where we were going.

When we parked near the Eiffel Tower, it was lit, and I almost gushed about how excited I'd be if we were going to the top of it, but I'd learned my lesson. I'd let this one unfold without expectations.

Hand in hand we walked through a security check that was closed to everyone but us. We were met by a security guard as we entered. He escorted us to what looked like it also acted as a security checkpoint during the day. We waltzed through to a waiting elevator.

"How did you arrange all this?" I asked with giddy wonder.

He cocked his head to the side. "I have some pretty influential friends."

"I guess so."

The ride up wasn't as long as I thought. It ended at the second level. From there we were led to another, smaller elevator. As it flew up, my hold on Mauricio's hand tightened. I wasn't afraid of heights, but the combination of the speed and view was unnerving. He pulled me back against his chest, lending me the security of his embrace.

We stepped out onto a smaller area with a metal floor. It was enclosed with glass windows. We walked over to look down. Stunning. A visual feast. Romantic, but our security guard was right with us. We ignored him, though he did keep us from exploring what might have been on our mind otherwise.

Mauricio spun me in his arms and gave me a quick kiss before asking, "Want to go farther up?"

"Sure."

He remained with us as we climbed a flight of stairs to an open-air, protectively caged area and gasped at the beauty of the view. In all directions, the city shone. The wind blew my hair around wildly. I felt like I was flying even though my feet were securely planted. There was a champagne bar that was open just for us. We clinked our glasses and took a selfie in front of a sign that claimed that was the kissing spot. Despite our audience, I turned, threw my arms around Mauricio's neck, and gave him a kiss of sheer gratitude.

He groaned and kissed me back with matching hunger. It was a kiss that would have taken us all the way had we been anywhere else. A difficult kiss to end, but we did.

"I'm glad you approve of this tour," he said lightly.

"How could I not?" I felt like I was dreaming. "I will never forget tonight. Never."

Hands on my hips, he said, "There's more. The tour isn't over yet."

"No?" I didn't care if it was. I would have gone home with him right then. "What else is here? The restaurants?"

"Better than that," he promised and led me toward another staircase.

The security guard went up the stairs before us to open the door. As we followed him, I realized where we were headed. "Eiffel's apartment?"

"Oh yeah," Mauricio said, once again looking pleased with himself.

A slow smile spread across my face. The geek in me was having an intellectual orgasm. We stepped inside the small apartment. It was musty, cramped with old furniture and wax figures of Eiffel, his daughter, and Thomas Edison—the most perfect, romantic spot I could have ever imagined. "This is where Eiffel met with scientists of his time. No one was allowed in unless he invited them. Do you feel their energy? I do." I didn't dare touch so much as a tabletop. Everything there was too precious, too valuable.

"What topic would you have chosen had you met him? If he was here now?" Mauricio asked.

It was a deep question and one that I took a moment to consider before answering. "I would have asked him how he chose his projects. When everyone told him the Eiffel Tower was ugly, how did he shut out the noise? Did he ever doubt himself, or was his path clearly set before him?"

Arm around my waist, Mauricio said, "I would have liked to hear his answers. I've asked myself those same questions."

My gaze flew to meet Mauricio's. "You have?"

He looked around the room, then met my gaze again. "I've spent the last several years working for my family's company. Where we took it was mostly my brother Sebastian's dream. I stepped up when I had to, gave him the reins when he could handle them. For a while, I was where I needed to be. He's in a better place now, and I'm free to do something on my own if that's what I want."

I completely understood that feeling. "I have enough in my savings that I could leave my job and take a position where I actually get to do something. My role right now is more about inspecting and documenting. I've always wanted to create something."

"What would you create?"

"See, that's the problem. I don't know." I sighed and scanned the diagrams in frames on the wall. "Do you think he always knew this was what he wanted to do, or did it just drop into his lap?"

Mauricio was quiet for a moment. He searched my face with an intensity I didn't understand, then tucked a strand of my hair behind one of my ears. "I bet it took him completely by surprise. He wasn't looking for it, didn't feel ready, but once he saw the potential of it, no other path seemed right."

In this emotionally charged moment I felt a deep connection with a man who was still a stranger to me on so many levels. How was that possible?

The guard asked if we were ready to go. We reluctantly said we were. I could have stayed there forever, but I knew the value of even our short visit. "I'm ready. Thank you."

We made our way back down to the open part of the summit. I touched the railing, still unable to believe Mauricio had done this for me. I searched his face. Would a man go this far for a woman he wouldn't remember next week? Would I feel this much for a man if the connection wasn't real? No one could be that good an actor—and if he could be, why would he go to this extent? "I've already slept with you," I blurted out.

His eyebrows shot up to his hairline; then he jokingly wiped a hand across his forehead. "Thank God you reminded me. I had forgotten about that."

A panic I couldn't explain nipped at me. "This doesn't make sense."

He leaned against the railing next to me. "Which part? That I didn't know there were creepy mannequins in the Eiffel apartment? That I didn't realize our security buddy would take his job quite so seriously?"

I glanced over to where the guard was watching us from only a few feet away. I'd forgotten about him. "I loved every minute of tonight. No one has ever done anything like this for me. Ever. I've gotten flowers.

A jade ring once. Men have taken me to the movies. Out for pizza. I thought having steak was special."

"You've been dating the wrong men."

I looked around again and felt a little overwhelmed. "This is a lot. I don't know what it means."

He raised both hands in mock surrender. "Does it have to mean anything more than I want to be with you?"

As I struggled to articulate how I was feeling, I once again found it difficult to breathe. I wanted this to mean he wanted to be with me. I wanted how he made me feel to be real. I also didn't want to charge forward when he wasn't charging with me.

I'm a coward.

I'm never going to leave the job I hate.

I'm going to ruin this, then marry some man I don't even want to sleep with.

Or die alone.

I don't want to die alone.

Mauricio turned to the guard. "We should probably get her back to the ground."

He nodded in agreement.

I followed Mauricio and the guard down the stairs and into the elevator. Mauricio had taken me to Eiffel's apartment. He'd given me a memory that would overshadow anything I'd find back home.

We went from one elevator to the next without speaking. When we stepped back out into the night, beneath the center of the Eiffel Tower, I turned to him and said, "I'm sorry. I didn't mean to freak out back there."

He put an arm around my waist. "I get it. A lot of people don't like heights."

I wished that had been it. I tapped my temple. "Sometimes I over-think things."

"You don't say . . ."

"Stop. I'm being serious. I get a thought in my head, and it just kind of circles around."

He pulled me into his arms. "I'm the same way. I pictured you naked a few minutes ago, and now it's all I can think about."

I gave him a long look. There I was contemplating mortality, and he was thinking about sex?

He kissed my neck, and I forgot what I was worrying about. There was only him, the wonder of his kiss, and then the security guard inviting us to continue our date anywhere else. Mauricio thanked him like they were old friends, and if our behavior had annoyed the man, he no longer seemed bothered by it. He waved to us as we left through the security entrance.

Outside the car Mauricio had waiting for us, we paused. Mauricio bent down to my ear and said, "Come back to my place, Kitten."

Someone once said that being brave doesn't mean never being scared—it means doing what's right despite being afraid. I'm not sure they were talking about deciding to have a second night of amazing sex despite how it might lead to eventual heartbreak, but it gave me the strength I needed to say, "Oh God, yes."

He kissed me then—with the kiss I'd expected. All sex and promises. Decadent. Demanding.

Perfect.

CHAPTER SEVENTEEN

MAURICIO

There is a clarity that hits a man post orgasm. As my breathing returned to normal, I began to think we might both be more comfortable in my bed rather than spending the rest of the night on the cold wooden conference table we'd finished on. I reluctantly disentangled from Wren and rolled off the table to stand. Giving in to a romantic side of me I was only just realizing I had, I scooped Wren up and carried her to where she belonged—my bed.

I threw back the covers, laid her down gently, then joined her. It felt right to have her there, so right I kept my thoughts to myself. Tonight I didn't want her to bolt.

A smart man knows when not to rock the boat. My efforts had given me a second chance with her, and I'd made the most of it. If that woman could now look at a crepe without thinking about me going down on her while she ate one, my name wasn't Mauricio Romano.

Four orgasms. That had to be enough even for my Kitten. Myself, I'm normally sated at two, but for her I'd rallied and shown her not only the joy that could be found on the balcony while overlooking the city, but also in the shower, and all over the meeting room of the penthouse. Come on, what other man would have been considerate enough to plan crepes to be delivered mid–sex marathon?

I wrapped my arms around Wren, loving how she snuggled closer as I did. This time she wasn't going anywhere.

She traced my chin with one of her deliciously talented fingers. "That was incredible."

"You're welcome," I said with a smug smile.

She pinched my chest lightly, playfully. "I'm too weak to think of a good comeback for that, but once my brain starts functioning again, watch out."

I kissed her gently on the lips before saying, "Then my only choice is to keep you constantly dazed from too many orgasms."

She chuckled; then her expression turned serious. "Thank you for tonight." She placed her finger over my lips to keep me quiet. "Yes, for the great sex, but I'm also talking about the Louvre and the Eiffel Tower. They're memories I'll never forget. Never. It was all pure magic, and I just want you to know how grateful I am." I opened my mouth to say something, but she stopped me with a look. "Don't make a joke. This is probably all routine to you, but it isn't for me."

I kissed her finger, then took her hand in mine, lowering it to my chest. "Nothing about us is routine to me."

She chewed her bottom lip before saying, "I think I'll be okay if we don't talk about Saturday. I want to enjoy this time with you. And when it's over, I want to be okay with it. I don't want to be angry or hurt. I panic sometimes. I'm not proud of it. I'm beginning to see that it holds me back. I'm trying to work on it. Can we do that? Can we just have fun this week?"

"Absolutely." I was tempted to tell her I was looking for more than just fun with her, but she didn't look ready to believe me. I decided the best way to prove to her that I wanted more than until Saturday with her was to remain in her life afterward. Simple. If overthinking things sent her into a panic, then we wouldn't think about it . . . we'd just do it.

She laid her head on my shoulder and closed her eyes. "Guess what I realized today."

"What?"

"Crazy-small underwear feels like a perma-wedgie. I don't know if I'm the lingerie type."

I chuckled, unable to look away from the woman I was beginning to wonder how I'd ever lived without. "With my expert help, I'm sure we can find something that not only looks good, comes off easily, but is also enjoyable for you to wear."

She opened one eye to peer at me. "Comes off easily? That's something I never considered when buying clothing."

"Really? Then let me add to your wardrobe. It's a matter I've put serious thought into." With a grin, I said, "Not that I have any complaints about what you've worn so far."

She yawned and closed her eyes. "Good save at the end."

I kissed her forehead. "What do you want to do tomorrow?" My first option would have been to stay right where we were, but I knew she wanted to see more of Paris. "We could helicopter over to Versailles. The Champagne region is a little farther, but also very doable. You pick and I'll make it happen."

She half opened her eyes. "Catacombs? You can say no. They aren't for everyone, but I've read so much about them, and I'm really curious. Solving a seventeenth-century health problem by relocating the remains of six million Parisians into old limestone quarries—now that was an engineering feat that changed lives. Some of the tunnels were already collapsing. It took real courage to take on that project. I'd like to see how it turned out."

I'd offered her expensive, luxurious options. She wanted a cheap tour of skulls and bones decoratively piled in tunnels beneath the city. At least that was how I'd always thought of the catacombs until she'd described them. Now I wanted to see more of the world through her eyes. "Done."

She fell asleep then.

I didn't. I held her close, stared up at the bedroom ceiling, and smiled as I replayed our date in my head. I'd come to Paris looking for who I once was. I hadn't expected to meet someone who would make me want to be more than I'd ever been.

Two days shouldn't be enough to know.

I smiled again. My father would argue that when it was right, it didn't even require that much time.

The last thought I had before I succumbed to sleep was that I wanted to learn more about her parents. Did they need a cow?

CHAPTER EIGHTEEN

———

WREN

I woke to a burned smell. It took me a moment to figure out where I was. Mauricio, wearing only boxer shorts, was standing beside the bed with a tray of food in hand. If it weren't for his super-pleased-with-himself smile, I would have thought I was dreaming. Have I mentioned how beautiful he was? He had the kind of abs a woman wanted to reach out to touch even though she had already kissed every inch of them.

And those shoulders. Ooh la la. He reminded me of the actor who plays Thor, and I'd watched every movie he'd been in just for scenes when he bared his chest. I'd seen *Aquaman* a few times as well for a similar reason. *I guess I have a thing for chests.*

"Morning, Kitten. Hungry?"

I took another moment to savor his perfection and felt a rush of heat when the front of his boxers tented in response to my perusal. "I am," I said in what I hoped was a sexy morning-after voice.

"Sit up, then."

As I did, the bedding fell away, revealing my bare breasts. I almost pulled the sheet up to cover myself, but I liked the feel of his gaze on them. With him, I felt beautiful and free. I left the sheet where it was, scooted over so he could sit beside me, then helped him settle the tray onto my lap. There were croissants, eggs, a carafe of coffee, two cups, and a muffin. Not one of them looked charred. I decided not to ask. "Breakfast in bed. Impressive."

He leaned in and kissed me. "You bring out a side of me I didn't know I had."

I rolled my eyes. That was probably his go-to line. "Well, it all looks delicious."

He settled in next to me. "I had it sent up from the hotel's kitchen. My attempt had to hit the trash. I may have overestimated how long bread takes to toast."

I arched an eyebrow at him. "You don't know how to make toast?"

He poured us each a cup of coffee. "I've seen it done, just never had to do it myself. Tell me you're a good cook."

"I can make toast," I parried.

"And?" he asked in an oddly hopeful tone.

"And when I'm home I have several local restaurants on speed dial."

He chuckled. "You're joking, of course."

I accepted the coffee he held out for me with narrowing eyes. I wasn't inept in the kitchen, but I didn't like the implication that it would matter if I were. "Why would I joke about not being able to cook? Do you think everyone with a vagina naturally knows how? Or even wants to?"

He cocked his head and studied me. "You know how to cook, don't you? But you're just giving me shit."

I picked up a croissant and bit into it before answering. "I guess that depends how important you think that skill is for a woman. Do you think cooking is a woman's role?"

He bit into the muffin and chewed without answering. Finally he said, "This is what I call a land mine conversation. I think I know what you want me to say, but I don't know what kind of baggage you're bringing to the table. So I have to tread carefully to make it out alive."

I was about to tell him I didn't have baggage, but if I did I knew a place he could shove it; then he winked, and my heart melted. I decided to be honest rather than defensive. "I grew up with two hard-working parents. They shared the chores, took turns cooking, doing laundry—everything. A real partnership that wasn't dependent on socially mandated gender roles. My mother knows how to change a spare tire and my father can make a quiche."

He gave me a long look. "I currently have a cook who prepares my meals, but before that my mother wouldn't let any of us set foot in her kitchen. My father may know how to scramble eggs. I'm not sure. I've never seen it. They're happy, though."

"So your baggage is old-world style," I said in a dry tone. "Might be time to update it."

His smile was quick and easy. "The problem is I love to eat."

I couldn't help but smile back. "Have you considered learning how to cook?"

"Anything is possible with the right teacher." His eyes lit with a mix of laughter and desire. "Speaking of teaching, I have to say I was impressed with your balance when we tried that position in the shower. I thought for sure you'd fall."

I laughed. "I trusted you wouldn't let that happen."

"I would have at least tried to catch you, but you were soapy and slippery. It could have gone either way."

I threw a piece of my croissant at him.

He tossed it back at me, then ducked in for a kiss.

We both sat back with a happy smile and continued munching on our breakfast choices.

How was it possible that I hadn't known this man more than a few days? If I hadn't gone to Paris, I never would have met him. If I'd decided to meet Cecile in a restaurant rather than Felix's apartment, I might never have run into Mauricio at all during this trip.

My heart started to pound.

How could anything that felt so much like it had been meant to be have come from a set of random decisions?

I shook my head and told myself not to overthink this. How close we'd come to never meeting, as well as how long we'd be together, were both topics that would only tear down the joy I was feeling that morning. Temporary or not, I wanted to enjoy my time with Mauricio.

I couldn't have asked for a nicer, sexier, better-looking man to have a fling with in Paris. If I ruined this week for myself, it would be something I'd always regret.

Maybe that was the beauty of a fling . . . maybe nothing this good was meant to last. Like a bouquet of flowers. Or the perfect spring day. Knowing that they would soon be gone made them that much more special. That was how I told myself to see my time with Mauricio.

Magical. Fleeting.

I picked a crumb off my left breast and placed it on the tray. When I looked up, I caught Mauricio laughing.

"You could have left it—a snack for me for later."

"Food and sex. I see a pattern with you."

He leaned over, took one of my nipples in his mouth, and slowly circled it with his tongue. That was all it took for my body to hum for him again. He kissed his way to where the crumb had been, licked the spot, then sat back again. "Is that a problem?"

I put my coffee down with a clatter. "Not at all. I like food too."

I moved the tray to the table beside us. "And?" He removed his boxers and dropped them to the floor. He stood beside the bed; his cock was gloriously at full size. I rolled onto my knees and licked the tip of it.

"That's it. Just food. Why? Was there something else?" I asked huskily before taking him into my mouth, then running my tongue down the length of him as I eased him out.

He buried a hand in my hair, gripping it, holding me in place. "There might be more you should consider."

I took him into my mouth again, using my hand to extend the sensation of depth. With my lips tight around him, I moved up and down, pulling back to circle the tip of him before plunging him as deep as I could take him.

I brought him to the brink; then I pulled back, found a condom, and threw it at him. It wasn't subtle, but it gained me what I was craving. He donned it, rolled onto the bed with me, and began his own intimate tease. In his excitement, he was rougher, but not more rushed. His skilled fingers got me as ready as he was. His mouth adored mine, my breasts, my stomach, and lower.

When he finally thrust into me, I called out his name and begged him not to stop.

Then no words, no thoughts, were possible in the face of being taken by him. When he growled "Mine" in my ear, I felt like his. I cried out that I was. Deeper. Fuller. Faster. Harder. We rode the waves of pleasure until they brought us to a sweaty, panting, sated mutual crash.

"Do you want your vibrator?" he whispered.

"Are you trying to kill me?" I whispered back. "I've come so many times in the past two days I'm surprised I'm still capable of speech. My brain is mush."

We shared a laugh and stayed exactly where we were, still joined, with me draped across him. He kissed my temple. "You say that like it's a bad thing."

A thought came to me and popped out of my mouth before I had time to filter it. "How many times do you think it's possible for a person to come in one day?"

He rolled me off him, cleaned off, and returned with my toy. "For the sake of science, I think we should answer that question." He turned it on and held it lightly against the lip of my sex, just enough for me to feel the vibration of it. "Unless you'd rather go to the catacombs."

I spread my legs and gasped in anticipation. "The catacombs can wait until tomorrow. I mean, this is for science."

He dipped my toy inside me, and a beautiful warmth spread through me. He lay on his side next to me and ran his hand leisurely over my body as the vibrations he controlled brought me ever-increasing pleasure.

Once.

Twice.

Three times.

I asked for a glass of water before the fourth.

We cuddled before the fifth.

Each was different. Some intense. Some more subtle. The sixth one ended with me feeling light headed and overdone. I called a halt when he would have started again a few minutes later.

"Six," I said in a bit of a daze. "That's my limit."

"Seven if you count the one we had together; don't undervalue your stamina."

I raised a weak hand at him and smiled. *Seven.* "I love Paris."

"Paris? That was all me, honey." He paused, then tossed my toy to the side. "Well, me with the help of your little buddy there. I guess you could name it Paris if you want."

Do people name their vibrators? I didn't have the strength to ask the question aloud. Never had I felt so relaxed, so much like I could simply float off the bed.

I closed my eyes—basking in the feeling of oneness with the universe and Mauricio. I'd never tried drugs, but what we'd just done had definitely been mind-altering . . . in the most amazing way.

In the distance I heard his phone ring, then felt the bed shift as he went to answer it. "Early afternoon. I meant to. I'm sorry." If I'd had the energy, I would have rolled over to ask him who he was talking to, but I was too relaxed. "I haven't called because there was nothing to share. Yes. No. Please don't. I love you too. Goodbye."

I love you too?

I sat up in bed. "You're married."

He crawled back onto the bed after tossing the phone onto the bedside table. "Worse, I'm a man with overprotective parents. I didn't call them yesterday, and it freaked them out."

I searched his face and replayed the conversation I'd overheard in my head. "That's the truth?"

He propped himself up on his elbows. "Have I ever lied to you?"

I wanted to say no, but I answered more honestly. "I don't know. I'd like to think you haven't."

He frowned. "I'd like to think you'd be more sure."

It was difficult to think, but I mustered some of my faculties. "We just met a few days ago. And your friend Felix was a real ass to Cecile."

He rubbed a hand over his face. "I know. I heard. He's not normally like that, but there were extenuating circumstances. Ones I'm not free to discuss."

I would have had more of an opinion on that, but I was really, really relaxed. "I can't imagine anything that would excuse slamming a door in someone's face, but we don't have to talk about it now. We don't have to talk about it at all."

He looked torn for a moment, then pulled me back down into his arms. "I vote for that." His smile took the sting out of his words.

I settled against him, the beat of his heart loud in my ear. "I want to trust you, Mauricio."

He nuzzled my hair. "Trust takes time, Kitten. You're right. You're pretty smart, you know that?"

As always, he'd said exactly what I wanted to hear.

I almost wished he hadn't.

Perfect meant it wasn't real.

CHAPTER NINETEEN

MAURICIO

The next morning I followed Wren down what felt like an endless spiral of stairs. So many I joked, "It's a long way down to the gates of hell."

She paused and looked over her shoulder at me. "I don't see it that way at all. I wonder who drew the diagram for this stairway. How did they determine the width, the materials . . . when they laid down the first step . . . how certain were they that it would stand the test of time?"

The railing was metal. The column in the middle looked like concrete. "It seems reasonably modern."

She ran her hand along the painted wall. "Which is just as impressive. Someone was entrusted with the challenge of making something accessible that wasn't meant to be. And they did it. I'm already impressed."

So was I. I wouldn't want to see the catacombs with anyone else. With her, we weren't making our way down a graffiti-riddled stairway—we were bearing witness to someone's achievement. She made me see how much more enjoyable the world was when it wasn't taken for granted.

Sidewalks? Someone had to think of designing them.

The pedestrian lights were more than an annoying device that one had to wait on; they were a modern marvel designed to save lives.

And she wasn't just a woman. She was one I'd woken up beside multiple times and one I wanted to wake up next to tomorrow.

And the day after.

And all the days that followed.

I had no idea it was possible to feel this much for someone I hadn't known very long.

More importantly, I'd never felt so much for any woman—regardless of our length of acquaintance.

Wren was it—my one.

The enormity of that revelation was next-level unsettling. We were leaving Paris the next day, and I still hadn't decided how to not get on separate planes. Could I convince her to come home with me? Did I ask to go back with her?

She started walking again, and we made our way into an area with photos and some of the history of the catacombs. I listened to her read the blurbs, but my attention wandered. Hopefully there wouldn't be a quiz at the end of this tour, because I was more focused on the beauty of the woman before me than the method that had been employed to transport bones.

Bodies moved at night?

There were other things I'd rather imagine happening in the night.

Eventually organized?

I had some organizing to do for tomorrow. When I told her how I felt, I didn't want to simply blurt it out. It would likely be a moment she'd treasure. It should happen somewhere special.

I could have someone at the airport simply escort her to my plane instead of hers. That was how every romantic movie I'd been forced to sit through would have done it. Some grand gesture followed by a declaration.

I wasn't planning a ring-exchanging moment, but it would still be a pivotal conversation for us. Tomorrow I'd show her that what we had didn't have an expiration date.

I continued to follow her through one empty narrow tunnel after the next. So far the place wasn't living up to the hype. Wren exclaimed now and then about something she saw through a grate. I tossed out comments in support, but not because I was paying attention to where we were.

My place or hers. My parents or hers first. The perk of having a private plane was that we could change our route accordingly.

I realized just then that I didn't know where she lived.

I didn't even know her last name.

How had I not circled back for that? Our time together had flown by so quickly. Still, that was something I should have known. I pictured introducing her to my parents without it. "Mom, Dad, this is Wren. Wren who? Oh, who the fuck knows. We just met in Paris. We haven't gotten around to things like last names yet."

We should start with her parents.

Her hand laced with mine, and she clung to it while looking around. "It's humbling, isn't it?"

"What?"

She gave me a look that said she hoped I was joking. I smiled to give myself a moment to catch up on whatever I was missing. We had walked into an area flanked with what looked like leg bones stacked one on top of the others almost to the ceiling. Skulls were decoratively placed in a variety of designs, both on the sides and on top. *Oh, shit. The scene belonged in a horror movie. Or a mortician's nightmare.* "Humbling. Yeah, that's the word I was looking for."

She pulled me farther through the catacombs to where we saw skulls positioned in the shape of a heart. She paused there and studied it. "Do you think whoever did that went home and told his wife he'd spent the day thinking of her? He wouldn't have taken a photo of it, but maybe he brought her back to see it."

I made a face. "That's one way to get laid."

She hip checked me. "Or maybe it was a tribute to someone he loved and lost." She looked around. "I thought coming here would make me sad, but it wasn't like these people were murdered. Each of them lived a life . . . whatever life they'd been destined for. No, they aren't buried separately, but we don't live separately, do we? Our lives are just as tangled together and interdependent as that wall of bones. No one is an island. There's a beauty to this place I didn't expect."

I pulled her back against me, linking my hands in front of her stomach. I don't know if I'd go as far as saying the tunnels were beautiful, but even I couldn't joke in the face of this display of departed humanity. "I wonder how many of them thought they'd live forever."

She leaned back into my embrace. "I bet all of them at one time. It's the quirk of our existence. We know that everyone who came before us ended up just like this, but we rush through life certain there will be time to do everything. Tomorrow isn't guaranteed. I wonder how many of them felt they'd lived their life on their terms and how many left wishing they had done everything differently."

I kissed the side of her head. Her words renewed my conviction to follow my heart with her and trust that doing so would lead me to the answers I was looking for. I pointed at one of the skulls. "When that guy died, I bet no one applauded him for how much money he had in his bank account."

She smiled up at me, then pointed at another skull. "He worked hard to support his family, but he also made time for them. That's not easy."

Even though I knew nothing about the history of the bones before me, I pointed to another skull and said, "Now this woman, she had the heart of a doctor back when no one believed women could. I bet she saved a lot of lives without ever getting recognition for it."

She glanced up at me again, visibly pleased with my guess. She pointed to another. "See the missing hunk of skull on that one? He didn't meet a good end."

"He deserved it. What an asshole."

She laughed and turned to kiss me on the cheek. "You're a funny guy."

"That's not what I want on my epitaph."

She waved a finger. "Let me guess . . . you'd like: well hung."

I nuzzled her hair and moved my hardening cock against her backside. "No need to make everyone else feel bad that they weren't born as well endowed as I was. No, I was thinking more along the lines of . . ." I stopped. "How did we get on such a morbid subject?"

She waved a hand around toward the skulls.

Oh yeah, right.

I took her by the hand. "Let's keep this tour going. I mean, I love mountains of human remains as much as the next person, but I've heard there are other, equally romantic spots in Paris. Some of them even have food."

She chuckled. "You and your stomach. How are you not fat?"

"Sex is a great calorie burner."

She rolled her eyes, but she was still laughing.

We made our way through the rest of the tunnels with a minimum of comments, then up another stairway to the gift shop, because even the catacombs end in one. I held up a lollipop and waved it at Wren. "Hey, is it just me or did seeing all those bones leave you with a craving for a candied skull?"

She shook her head but countered by holding up a skeleton snow globe. "No?"

"No." I took her hand again, and we walked out onto the street. "Last day in Paris. What would you like to see?" Feeling inspired, I asked, "Have you been to the Pont des Arts?"

She shuddered. "I'm sorry. I know the bridge of locks is supposed to be romantic, but I cringe at the idea of people selfishly destroying an ancient structure just because they want to hook a lock on it. People are crazy. How is that love? And they know the locks can't stay there forever. Someone will have to cut them off to save the bridge. So their gesture of showing how eternal their love will be . . . is really a demonstration of the opposite. What happens to them a couple months later when their lock is pried off the failing bridge?"

Yes, this was the woman for me. "They go from being completely in love to suddenly experiencing a sensation of being cut away from each other and tossed aside?"

"Yes!" She threw her free hand in the air as she spoke. "If a man wanted to show me our love was forever . . . I'd hope he'd be smart enough to build something rather than tear something down."

Build something?

What the hell did I know how to build?

"Yeah."

She blushed. "Sorry. What a ridiculous topic to get on. You asked me what I wanted to do tonight. How about just walking around Paris, maybe by the Seine. I'd love to see where we end up, eat at a restaurant we come across by chance, then . . .."

My body came to full attention. "Then?"

"Then whatever happens . . . happens." Her sex smile was one I knew well—equal parts innocence and bravado.

I spun her into my arms. "I hear that whatever happens, often happens more than once."

Her face was happy and glowing as she smiled up at me. "I've heard the same."

I kissed her then, as people walked past, and loved how she wound herself around me. Every old memory I had of Paris faded away. This would be how I'd remember the city—this feeling, this woman.

We started walking again, and there was a lightness in my step that hadn't been there in years. I was confident that however I chose to tell her how I felt, things would work out. Her parents. My parents. Her job. My current lack of one. We'd figure it all out.

After one more day in Paris.

And one more night in the penthouse.

CHAPTER TWENTY

———

Wren

I woke early the next morning in the warm comfort of Mauricio's embrace. He was still asleep, and I took advantage of the opportunity to simply appreciate the lines of his face.

Today is the day we end it.

How will that go?

Would he drive with me to the airport? Kiss me one final time before the security checkpoint?

Am I supposed to leave before he wakes? Save us both from that awkward final goodbye?

I've never had a fling. I don't know the rules.

Do I thank him?

I let out a shaky breath. *I don't want to leave.*

I don't want this to be over.

I wiped a tear from the corner of my eye. *I don't want to cry in front of him either.*

The whole week had been perfect. He'd been so wonderful. I couldn't be angry with him for not wanting more than we'd agreed to.

If my heart was hurting, I'd done that to myself.

My phone beeped from the table beside the bed. I leaned over to check it. There was a message from my mother asking me to call her when I woke up. I'd sent her my itinerary and updates. She might have wanted to tell me she was excited I was coming home.

I slipped out from under Mauricio's arm, pulled his shirt over my head, and headed into the other room with my phone, closing the door behind me as I went. I called her as soon as I was out of earshot of the bedroom. "Hi, Mom. What's up?"

"I'm sorry, Wren. I know you're coming home today." Her voice was thick with emotion. "Everything is probably going to be fine, but if there's any way you could get on an earlier flight, could you?"

I swayed on my feet. My mother was the least needy person I knew. If she thought she needed me, it was for something serious. "What happened?"

"Remember Dad's old army buddy, Trev?"

"Yes."

"He died yesterday. Your dad left after he got the call. Flat out left. I checked the garage. No one has seen him. I called every bar. God, I even called hospitals. No one has seen him. He left his phone here. I'm scared, Wren. Trev was the one who pulled him out of his depression after he lost his arm. I don't know what to do. Should I call the police?"

I sat down on a stuffed chair and processed what my mother was saying. I didn't want to consider the worst-case scenario, but I had to. My father had battled with PTSD for my entire life. He tried to hide it from my mom and me, but if he saw something in the news or heard someone say something, it could trigger him into depression. He'd retreat to the garage, tinker with an engine, and hide from us. Normally, he needed only a few hours.

Once, when I was in high school, he'd tried to help a friend fix his car and somehow had dropped an engine block on the man's foot. Although he'd been sober during the accident, that night was the first time I'd ever seen my father drunk. Mom had picked him up from a bar, and after tucking him in bed, we'd talked. She'd explained that when my father had been injured he hadn't been alone. His truck had been part of a convoy. When the explosion had gone off, he'd been thrown far enough that the second explosion had missed him. Awake, and not yet aware that he'd lost his arm, he'd watched his friends die without being able to help them.

And a piece of him had died with them.

I didn't want to ask, but I had to know . . . "Did he take his gun with him?"

"Oh my God. You don't think—"

"Just look, Mom. Make sure it's there."

She was crying when she returned. "It's here." She let out a sob, then sniffed. "I'm so sorry, Wren. I know you never take vacations, and this is a pretty crappy way for your trip to Paris to end."

"Paris doesn't matter, Mom. I'm glad you called me." I took a fortifying breath. I wanted to cry right along with my mother, but she needed me to be strong. I'd cry later. "Everything is going to be okay. I'll grab my stuff, head to the airport, and catch the first flight I can. Call Dave Stein. His brother is a police officer. He might be able to help us find Dad without making this bigger than it has to be. Dad might have just needed some time to himself to mourn his friend. Where would he go besides the garage?"

"I don't know. He's never left without telling me where he was going, Wren. Never. I should have gone with him. I almost did. I just thought . . . Wren, hurry home."

I was on my feet gathering my clothes and everything of mine that was scattered around the penthouse. "I will, Mom. I'll call you as soon as I have a flight."

After hanging up, I crept into the bedroom. Mauricio was still sound asleep, with his arm flung out over the spot I had vacated. I almost woke him up. This was big, and I could have used his support.

But we're not a couple.

He's a fling, not a shoulder to lean on.

Saying goodbye to him that day had already involved the risk of me dissolving into sloppy tears; he'd done nothing to deserve the full meltdown I was now capable of. Creeping out while he slept was actually the kindest thing I could do in the situation.

I grabbed my clothing, dressed quietly, and lifted my luggage off the floor, closing the door of the bedroom behind me. I paused at the kitchenette. There was a pen and paper. *I should write something so he doesn't worry.*

I wrote: *Thank you for an amazing week. —Wren*

It didn't represent how I was feeling, but it was the best I could do in the situation. I needed to get the rest of my things from my original place, get to the airport, and find my dad. I couldn't give myself the luxury of feeling one way or another about leaving without one final kiss.

· Later—once my father was safely back at our home and I knew he was okay—later, I'd acknowledge how my heart was breaking. How I'd felt like I was walking away from the one man I'd ever let into my heart.

As I rode down the elevator, I was already searching online for any flight that left earlier than mine did. I found one, paid a crazy amount of money to switch to it, and sent the info to my mother before I was even at my apartment. The rest of the morning was a flurry of throwing everything into my luggage, locking up, texting the rental agency to inform them that I was out, and rushing to make my flight.

It wasn't until I was seated on the plane and we'd left the ground that I burst into tears. The older gentleman next to me handed me tissues and, after I assured him I was fine, pretended I didn't cry on and off most of the eight-hour flight home.

CHAPTER TWENTY-ONE

MAURICIO

Thank you for an amazing week. —Wren

No matter how many times I read it, I couldn't believe she'd left without saying goodbye. I'd reached for her when I'd first woken, called for her when I didn't see her, finally texted her—nothing.

When I'd first realized she wasn't in the penthouse, I'd thought she might have sneaked out to get food for us. I'd brought her breakfast in bed. It wasn't inconceivable that she might want to surprise me with something special that morning.

Oh, she'd fucking surprised me.

I'd found the note. At first, stupidly, I didn't instantly see it for what it was. She was grateful for the time we'd spent together and that explained why she'd run out to get something for me.

What a fucking idiot I was.

Love makes men into brainless saps. I was proof of that.

A quick look around had provided enough supporting evidence for a sane man to see that she was gone. She'd taken everything of hers with her. Even her luggage.

She wasn't coming back.

I couldn't wrap my head around it.

We'd made love just a few hours before. It had been exactly the slow, sweet kind of sex a man has with a woman he's about to promise forever to.

Thank you for an amazing week.

What the fuck was that? Who leaves a note after what we'd shared? Was it possible that she'd felt nothing?

I tried to call her. Texted her again. No answer.

I collapsed onto the couch and lay there, just staring off into space as I replayed every conversation we'd had in my head. She'd never said a single thing about us being together after that day.

I was her Paris fuck.

My phone rang. I let it go to my messages. It rang again a moment later. Was it her? I sat straight up.

No.

My parents.

Fuck.

I can't do this right now.

They would only call back if I didn't answer. Naked and devastated, I slumped back onto the couch. "Morning, Dad."

His tone was light and cheerful. "I don't want to pry, but your mother is planning the family dinner for Sunday, and she asked if she should set a place for your lady friend."

"Dad—"

"You haven't been calling us. You're sleeping in. It doesn't take a genius to add two and two together. You made up with her, didn't you?"

"She's gone, Dad." I hated how gutted I sounded as I said it. "Can we not do this right now? I really don't want to talk about her."

My father's voice deepened. "Are you coming home?"

"I guess. Probably. I don't know. I haven't gotten that far in my head."

"What happened, son?"

I growled and punched my leg. "I thought she was the one, Dad. I'm so fucking stupid. I don't even believe in love—not for me. What the fuck was I thinking? I was planning . . . you don't even want to know how sure I was . . . and after only a few days. How delusional am I? All we did this week was fuck. I should not have been shocked by her note or the fact that she left while I was still sleeping. Let me read her note to you, so you can see what an idiot your son is. She said, and I'm reading it exactly as she wrote it . . . 'Thank you for an amazing week.' That's it. Oh, and she signed it. Nothing else. What the fuck is that?"

When I stopped ranting, I regretted sharing as much as I had with my father. In my life, I'd probably only heard him swear once, and I didn't want to give him a bad impression of Wren. She didn't deserve that.

I slapped myself in the forehead and forced myself to read her note again. Why the hell was I worried about what my father thought of a woman who obviously didn't give a shit about me? I growled. I still didn't like the idea that anyone would see Wren in a bad light.

I couldn't take back what I'd said about her. My hand fisted on my leg, and I made another sound born of frustration.

After a long silence, my father said, "I'm sorry it didn't work out, son."

I sighed. "Me too. I was going to tell her how I felt today. I already knew the first recipe I wanted Mom to teach her. Not that she would have cooked it for me. I probably would have ended up cooking it for her." I slammed my hand down on my thigh again. "Who needs someone like that, right?"

Neither of us said anything for several minutes. Finally he asked, "Have you tried to call her?"

"She's not answering."

"Give her time. Despite what your generation thinks, not everything in life is immediate. She might need time away from you to realize she wants to be with you."

I shook my head in disgust—disgust with myself. "Maybe. Thanks, Dad. Sorry I went off like that. She was just special . . . you know?"

"I know."

I sighed. "Could you tell Mom a much, much better version of this? Something that doesn't make Wren sound—"

"You think your mother and I didn't have sex before we were married? Oh, the stories I could tell you—"

"Please. Please don't." I shuddered, then said, "I don't want to rehash this a hundred times when I get home. And I shouldn't have said what I did. I thought she was the one, but apparently she didn't feel the same. She knows how to reach me. The next move is hers."

"Come home, Mauricio. I'll tell everyone you met someone nice, but you're not ready to talk about it. That's all they need to know." After a pause, he added, "And leave the colorful language in Paris. You know your mother doesn't like it."

There was comfort in that reprimand. "Thanks, Dad."

"It's going to be okay, Mauricio. Things have a way of working out the way they're supposed to."

"I don't have much faith in that philosophy this morning, Dad. But I'll fly back this afternoon as planned and see you in the morning."

"Text us when you take off."

"I will. See you tomorrow."

Much, much later that day, I was met in the US at the airport by both of my parents and all my siblings—every damn one of them, even Sebastian, his pregnant wife, and little Ava. After giving me a back-thumping hug, my father said, "We thought you might be hungry. So we moved family dinner to tonight."

Little Ava ran over and took me by the hand and said, "Uncle Mauricio, did you bring me an Eiffel Tower?"

"It's in my bag," I assured her. "It even lights up."

She clapped happily, and I swung her around in my arms. I might have been a complete idiot when it came to love, but I had the uncle thing down pat.

Still holding Ava, I looked around at my family, who'd met me at the plane even though they could have waited until the next day to see me, and my heart was a little less heavy. This is what we did—when one of us took a hit, we pulled together.

Wren would have loved my family.

And my family would have adored her.

Ava gave my face a pat. "Uncle Mauricio, you look sad."

I forced a smile. "Just tired." I flapped my free arm like a bird. "It was a long flight."

She laughed.

I ducked down so my mother could plant a kiss on my forehead and said, "Hi, Mom. What's for dinner?"

CHAPTER TWENTY-TWO

WREN

During my flight, I came up with a plan on how to find my father. It involved calling the credit card company to see if he'd charged anything. When I went to text my mother, I saw messages from Mauricio, but I scrolled past them. I couldn't face my guilt about how I'd left or this nearly overwhelming yearning to call him . . . if only to hear his voice one last time.

I sent a message to my mother asking her to call her credit card company. Before I landed, she'd texted me back that he'd gotten gas in Allentown, Pennsylvania. After that, I had a pretty good idea where he was headed.

There was no way to know for sure, but I trusted my instincts and, as soon as I landed, I bought a ticket for the closest airport to Trev's hometown. Exhausted, but driven by the need to confirm that my father was okay, I rented a car in that terminal and drove to Trev's house.

By the time I pulled up, it had grown dark, but there was a light on inside the house. I turned off the car and sprinted up the steps, took a deep breath, then rang the doorbell. The door opened. Trev's wife peered around the edge, with her two sisters behind her.

He has to be here.

"I was so sorry to hear about Trev, Daeshona."

She hugged me to her ample chest. "I know you are, honey." When she released me, her sisters each gave me the same warm greeting. This was my second family, the one we didn't see often but which meant more to us than blood relatives who lived closer. After my father's medical discharge from the army, Trev had been allowed extra leave. My mother said he'd even temporarily moved Daeshona closer to our family while my father recovered.

Eventually she'd convinced him to move back to where her sisters lived, but my father had often referred to Trev as a brother from another mother. Trev had been in that convoy the day my father lost his arm, and although neither of them spoke of that day, I knew it had given them a bond neither time nor distance had diminished.

I knew the answer before I asked the question, but a part of me held on to hope. "Have you seen my dad? Heard from him?"

Daeshona shook her head sadly. "Not after I spoke to him yesterday. I felt horrible about giving him the news on the phone, but—"

I shook my head and touched her arm. "Don't. I would have done the same. This isn't easy on you either."

She placed her hand over mine. "No, it's not." Her chin rose. "But we had some warning it was coming. He wouldn't let me talk about it with anyone, but the doctors had been watching a tumor in the back of his brain. It was inoperable, which—you know Trev—meant it didn't need to be worried about. He fell asleep in his favorite chair and never woke up. It's how he would have wanted to go. He got his way—one last time." She smiled even though there were tears in her eyes. "I bet his mother arranged for it to go smoothly. She always did spoil him."

I smiled and fought back my own tears. "Good men like that deserve a little spoiling now and then."

"Damn straight they do," she said, then shook her head as if trying to shake herself free of a weight. "Your father took the news hard, didn't he?"

I hesitated. I didn't want to add the weight of what I was going through onto her at such a difficult time. On the other hand, she loved my father too. And she might know where he'd be. "He left after your call. Didn't take his phone with him and didn't say where he was going. We checked with the credit card company, and he stopped for gas at a station in this direction." I swallowed hard. "I was hoping he'd be here."

She clasped her hands in front of her. "I'm sorry, honey. I haven't seen him."

I nodded. "It was a gamble. I just thought—"

Her sister stepped forward. "Didn't Trev and Elliot always go fishing up by Wildwood Park? They used to joke that one of them should buy a cabin there so they could both retire where the fishing was good?"

"I remember."

Daeshona wrinkled her nose. "Up there they drank beer more than they baited any hooks. They'd escape there to talk family matters without any of us hearing."

For as long as I could remember, my father had driven to see Trev a couple of times a year. Sometimes we went with him; sometimes he'd gone alone.

To fish, apparently.

"Is Wildwood Park close?" I'd flown, flown more, and driven. I was exhausted, but there was no way I was stopping before I found my father.

"About fifteen minutes from here. The park will be closed, but there is a boat dock where they often went." Daeshona gave me a landmark I could GPS.

I kissed her on the cheek. Hugged each of her sisters quickly. "I have to go—"

Daeshona opened the door for me. "If he's there, tell him our home is open to both of you. Don't go doing anything stupid like renting a hotel room for tonight. It would only offend me."

"I'll call you if it's not late. If he needs to be there, I won't want to rush him."

"You always were a smart girl," Daeshona said, and I gave her one last hug.

"Thank you. Can I ask . . . when . . ."

"The wake is two days from now. The funeral the next day."

I didn't promise her I'd be there . . . I couldn't promise anything.

The drive felt like hours, when in actuality it was only the quarter of an hour Daeshona had predicted. I nearly burst into tears when I saw my father's car parked on the side of the road. After pulling up behind it, I cut the engine and grabbed my phone.

I couldn't see him from the road. It was dark, but I lit the way with the phone's light. There was no sound coming from near the water. I didn't know what condition I might find him in, but I knew he needed me. I sagged with relief against a tree when I saw the outline of him sitting on the dock, shoes on one side of him, a case of beer at his other. I quickly texted my mother: Found Dad. He's fine. I'm going to talk to him. Will call you later with an update.

I didn't wait for her response. If she had any questions, I didn't have any answers yet.

I walked down a grass hill and onto the dock. My father didn't glance back to see who approached. He was lost in his own thoughts.

I took a seat beside him and just sat there. After a few minutes, I removed my own shoes, turned off the light on my phone, and dangled my feet into the water the same as he was doing. The moon was bright that night and reflected off the water just enough so I could see his face.

There were three empty beer cans beside him. An open can in his hand. He tossed a fresh one to me. I caught it, cracked it open, and took a long drink. I didn't normally like beer, but I needed something.

He turned back to look out over the water.

There were so many things I wanted to say to him, but I took another gulp of beer instead. He wasn't there because he didn't care how Mom and I felt. He'd lost his rock. I wanted to promise I would be that for him, but I didn't know what it was like to be in a war. I didn't carry the kind of scars he did, and I wasn't sure I had anything to say that would live up to what Trev would have.

So we sat there. I don't know for how long.

Could have been hours.

We just sat there, each nursing the beer we were holding but never reaching for another.

"It should have been me," my father said in a low tone. "I don't understand why it's never me."

I blinked back tears. I still didn't know what to say to that.

He continued, "When the images in my head would get too dark, when I couldn't sleep and the memories started mattering more than you or your mother—I'd come here. Trev understood. He was there that day, was tortured by the same memories. We'd sit right here and tell stories about every friend we lost that day. Once we got so drunk we couldn't drive back, so we slept here. Daeshona was angry with him. Angry with me."

"Or just worried for both of you."

He nodded. "That too."

We sat in silence for several minutes before he said, "I'm sixty years old, Wren. I haven't been the husband your mother deserved. I tried to do my best by you."

I shifted closer and linked my arm with his. "You won't hear either one of us complaining. We love you, Dad."

He made a guttural sound. "I forgot my phone. Your mother must be so worried."

"She's fine now. I told her I found you."

He let out a sigh. "I don't remember how I got here. When I received the call, I needed some air. I went for a drive. Next thing I knew I was here."

"You came to where you needed to be."

"Yeah, I guess I did." He gave my hand a pat. "I don't know what I'm going to do without him."

Life didn't come with instructions for how to handle the day my father needed my guidance. I didn't think I was strong enough to deal with something like this, but I didn't have a choice, so I found the strength. It was that simple. "You're going to come home and talk to someone about your feelings. We'll find someone at the VA or on our own. What you're going through is more common than you think, Dad. When good people see what you saw—it stays with them. Tonight we're staying with Daeshona."

"I can't do that to her."

"You do not want to offend her. Plus, she's worried about you. Follow me back to her place and reassure her that you're okay. Trev would want you to."

My father nodded and began to put his socks and shoes back on. "He'd kick my ass if he knew I'd worried her at all."

I smiled because it was true and began to put my own socks back on. "The wake is in two days. That gives us time to drive home, get Mom, and come back. We'll find a nice hotel nearby." I laced my shoes, then stood. My father did as well. His pained expression was clearly visible even in the shadows. I stepped forward and simply wrapped my arms around him, laying my head on his chest.

He didn't move at first, then hugged me close. "I'm sorry, baby."

I only hugged him tighter. "We've got this, Dad. You, me, and Mom. The Heaths are made tough."

He released me with a hint of a smile. "How did I get so lucky, Wren?"

"I ask myself the same thing, Dad. I know why you're still here—we need you."

We started back up toward our cars. He'd forgotten his beer down on the dock, but I didn't mention it. It was best left behind.

"How was your trip?" he asked.

"It was—it was—" I struggled to condense everything Paris had been into one word. I was able to talk to my parents about most things, but even on his best day my father wouldn't have handled hearing about Mauricio well. He never approved of anyone I dated, so the chance that he'd want even vague details about my Paris fling? *Yeah, no.* "Unforgettable."

"I'm glad. And your friend Cecile?"

That made me smile. Dad had never much approved of her either. "It was great to see her. She's doing really well in London. It was fun to get back together now that we're both adults. I'm really proud of how she went after her dreams and made them a reality."

He stopped near the driver's side of my car. "You've done the same."

"Yep." Visually inspecting fire sprinkler systems had never been a dream of mine, but as a rule I tried not to engage in conversations I knew wouldn't make a situation better. What Dad was dealing with was more immediate and important than how I felt about my employment. I opened the door of my rental and slid in. "I'll follow you, Dad. You know the way back better than I do." I didn't want to let him drive, but he hadn't had a drink in hours, and we couldn't leave his car there.

His hand rested on the top of the door. "Life isn't a race, Wren. Maybe she got there first, but you're still young. You have plenty of time to do whatever you want to do."

I nodded. "I know. And I will. Now I'll call Mom and tell her we're on our way to Daeshona's. I hope you're hungry, because you know she'll want to feed us."

"You're a better daughter than I deserve," he said in a low tone.

My heart broke for him. "You're wrong, Dad. I've got some serious grit, and I'm here because I know exactly how important family is. Who do you think taught me all that? You did. So don't you dare put my father down. He's my hero. Understand?"

His eyes shone with tears he'd never let fall. "Yes, ma'am."

I sniffed and reached out for the door handle. "Good, now get your ass in your car, because I'm exhausted."

He smiled and closed the door.

It would be a rough week, but I felt a lot better now that I knew where he was.

I called Daeshona as I drove and told her that I'd found my father. She said we'd better be on our way to her, because she and her sisters had set the table for us. I chuckled and told her what our plans were for the next few days.

God, I was tired, but I felt a million times better than I had when I'd heard my father was gone. A scare like that brought a person's priorities right back into focus.

Sure, my heart was breaking, but everyone was carrying the weight of something. I'd survive. And if it was at all within my power to make it so—my father would too.

After a pause, Daeshona said, "I spoke to your mother. She said you flew straight here from Paris. I've never been. Tell me, is it as beautiful as people say?"

I remembered the crowds, the homeless people, the smell of urine in the Métro . . . then Mauricio and kissing him on top of the Eiffel Tower. "It's a city, one with a lot of history and beautiful monuments, but like any trip it was really about who I was with."

"That sounds like you have a story you want to share."

I gripped the steering wheel, careful to turn when my father did. "I'm not ready to talk about it yet, but when I am . . . you'll be fanning your face . . . that is, if you think you can handle the truth."

"Oh, honey, I'm not your mama. I'd better get the whole story. What was his name?"

I hesitated before saying his name out loud. Did I really want to bring that much of him home with me? "Mauricio."

"That's a name I haven't heard you say before."

"I met him while I was there."

"And he was face-fanning worthy?"

"Oh yes."

She chuckled. "When do I get to meet him?"

I took a breath. "Never. It was great, but it was just . . ." *But what?* That was part of the problem. I didn't know what it had been. I realized I'd fallen several car lengths behind my father and sped up. ". . . not important. Honestly, I'm just glad I found Dad."

CHAPTER TWENTY-THREE

Mauricio

Several days later, my brother Christof sat across from me in my living room and looked me over with a critical eye. "Any intention of showering today?"

I sat back on the couch and scratched at the four-day growth on my chin. "I showered yesterday. Or maybe the day before that."

Christof had let himself in, claiming we needed to talk. It had sounded serious, so I dropped my plans for the day—I'm kidding, I hadn't done a fucking thing since coming home from Paris.

Except mope.

Which surprisingly enough I discovered I was gifted at.

I'd slept in each morning, discovered binge-watching multiple seasons of TV series could eat up an afternoon as well as an evening . . . which had brought me back to what I really wanted to do more of . . . sleep again.

Christof's eyebrows rose and fell as he looked around the room. "Five pizza boxes. Impressive."

"A man cannot live on beer alone."

He made a face. "Dad told us not to talk about Paris with you. So this is me judging you for handling it like a pussy but not talking about it."

I half smiled at that. "Thanks for the support."

He folded his arms across his chest. "I should let you wallow long enough to get fat. You've always been too good looking. Welcome to what dating is like for the rest of humanity. Sucks, doesn't it?"

"It's horrible." I patted my still-flat abs. My brother did fine with women, but I liked to give him shit. "I'll hit the gym later. Once is all it should take to get this washboard tight again."

Christof rolled his eyes.

I picked up the TV remote.

He leaned forward, took it out of my hand, and tossed it on the floor out of my reach. "No more TV. You're getting out into the world today. Get up. Go shower and shave. You're coming to the office."

I leaned back into the couch. "Not going to happen."

He threw a couch cushion at my head. "Get the fuck off the couch."

I deflected the pillow easily. "No."

He stood, took the seat cushion from his chair, and winged it at my head. Annoying, but I blocked it as well. "Go home, Christof. I'm fine."

He picked up a glass of water I'd poured for myself the day before but never drank. "Last warning."

"Don't do something you're sure to regret."

He made a show of pulling his hand back as if readying to toss the water. "Why? Is Mauricio feeling fragile? Does he need coddling?"

My chest puffed. "Don't fucking do it."

"Then get up."

I didn't.

Only a brother I'd held down and tickled until he pissed himself when we were children would have done what he did. He threw that water right in my face.

Then wisely put the length of the room between us.

I wiped the water from my face, jumped to my feet, and was after him.

Keeping the table between us as we circled, he said, "Punching me will not make you feel better."

161

"It might."

I vaulted over the table at him. He skirted to the other side of it, keeping the distance between us the same.

"Don't make me call Mom," he warned.

I advanced. He retreated. Across the room, my phone beeped with a message. "You texted her? Seriously? I'm going to have to beat your ass just for being a rat."

"That's not Mom. You know she doesn't text."

I froze. It could be anyone. There was no reason to believe it was Wren, but what if it was? Any irritation with my brother was forgotten as I sprinted over to the coffee table, where I'd left my phone.

It's probably not her.

I picked up my phone.

It's her.

Finally, five days later, something. I'm sorry.

Phone in hand, I sank back onto the couch and simply stared down at the message.

Christof came to sit beside me. "Is it her?"

"Yes."

"What did she say?"

"She's sorry."

"That's good, right?"

I shrugged. I'd spent the last few days convincing myself I'd imagined how I'd felt about Wren. No one could feel that strongly about someone they hardly knew.

We'd had nothing more than the fling she'd said she wanted.

"Aren't you going to answer her?" he asked.

I put the phone back down on the table and growled, "What would I say? 'It's okay'? It's not. The way she left told me everything I needed to know."

Christof let out a sigh. "Dad thinks you really like her."

"I did. More than liked."

"Seems to me, if I'd met a woman I more than liked, and she texted me . . . I'd at least answer her."

"That's where you'd be wrong. This experience has been eye-opening for me. In every relationship there is a kisser and a kissee. One person is always more invested than the other. I'm the one who has always been ready to walk away. And you know what? That's the better place to be. This feeling? This scenario? It blows. I get why you don't like to see me like this. I don't want to be this person either. That woman is my kryptonite. I don't sulk. I don't pine. And I'll be damned if I let her make me into a man who does."

"Wow, that's . . . intense."

I folded my arms across my chest. "Learn from my mistake, Christof. Don't give a woman the upper hand. If you're stupid enough to hand her your heart, you might as well have your balls removed at the same time. You'll be just as much less of a man when she's done with you anyway."

He made a face. "Okay. So you're not ready to text her yet. Got it. I'm still dragging you out of the house today. It's up to you how you look when I do."

I glared at him.

He held my gaze without blinking.

He really was a good brother. "I'm glad I didn't punch you."

"Me too," he said with a grin. "I would have had to mess up that pretty face of yours, and Dad would have had us both doing his yard work for weeks."

I smiled. Dad probably would have given us that punishment, and we would have accepted it despite our age. He never did anything unless it was what was best for the family. "Mom would have hated watching her garden go to shit under our care. Remember when you mowed right over her flowers?"

163

He laughed. "I was watching you do some ridiculous ninja move with a rake . . . and Dad's mower wasn't as responsive as I thought. I was hoping for a tighter turn."

With a stretch, I stood. "I'll be ready in about fifteen minutes. I should shave too."

"Take your time."

I paused and looked down at the darkened screen of the phone.

She's sorry.

About what?

How she left?

Or that she didn't feel more for me?

I knew I'd respond to her—for my own sanity if for no other reason. But not in front of Christof.

The shower and shave did lift my mood slightly. As I dressed, I remembered camping out at Sebastian's place when he'd needed us to. His devastation had been much deeper and had gone on for months. Understandable since he'd lost a wife and child.

Me?

I was just an idiot.

CHAPTER TWENTY-FOUR

WREN

I could have taken the whole week off from work, but the day after returning from Trev's funeral, Dad had gone back to work at the gas station. He had an appointment to talk to someone at the VA. Mom said they were both fine. It was time to stop hovering over them. We all needed to get back to our lives.

Dressed in jeans and an oxford shirt with the company logo, I sat in my truck in the parking lot of my next job, waiting for Mauricio to answer my text. I felt horrible about the way I'd left. I also didn't feel too good about how long it had taken me to apologize, but I'd gone into survival mode for the first few days back.

When I'd surfaced from that?

Well, I didn't think he'd want to hear from me.

Had he left while I'd slept, I wouldn't have been too receptive to hearing from him again. Sure, I'd had my reasons, but none that he knew of. I was torn between telling him or just letting things ride.

I couldn't not apologize, though.

Looking down at my message, I shook my head in disgust. I'm sorry.

Cryptic. Selfishly safe.

Not worth sending.

Probably only confusing to receive.

He hadn't texted back.

There weren't even those little dancing dots that show up when someone is typing a response.

I don't blame him. I didn't answer any of his messages. I gave him good reason to write me off.

Of course that's assuming he wasn't relieved when he woke up and I was gone.

Either way it's unfair to be upset with him. He delivered everything he'd promised.

For all I know Felix has already sent him to play interference with another woman, and he's taking her friend all over Paris . . . feeding her whatever her fantasy is in exchange for a week of sex.

Whoever she is—I hate her.

I laid my head down on the steering wheel and admitted I was a mess.

I'd known what we had was temporary.

I'd agreed to it.

Even if he answered me and wanted to continue our wild romance, I was firmly planted back in reality. Paris had been about stepping away . . . enjoying the freedom. It had also proven that what I'd always feared was a real possibility. All I had to do was look away, and I could lose everything.

If I hadn't called my mother . . .

If I hadn't found my father . . .

I took a deep breath and fought back the panic that nipped at me. *But I did find him. I couldn't have known Trev would die.*

It would have been just as bad even if I'd been there.

I told myself that again but didn't completely believe it. Guilt wasn't new to me—we were old companions. I felt bad about leaving. I felt worse about how much I'd enjoyed being away.

I wanted the comfort of Mauricio's arms, but I didn't want to have to explain why I needed the comfort . . . and I felt bad about that as well.

I was a mess.

I sighed and raised my head. Okay, so there were some things I had no control over. But there were some I did. I didn't have to continue to work at a job I didn't like.

I could quit.

Right then and there.

Start over. Build the life I wanted—within driving distance of my parents. There was no reason I couldn't.

I smacked the steering wheel as I gathered courage. "I'm doing it. I'm going to call my boss and tell him he needs to send someone else to check this site. I'm done." Saying it out loud made it real—scary, but real.

I was so lost in my thoughts that I screamed when someone knocked on my truck window.

It was an older man in a dark-gray suit. Dark eyes. Dark hair. He reminded me of Mauricio, but I saw Mauricio everywhere I looked lately. I shook my head to clear it and lowered my window. "Can I help you?"

His smile was easy and confident. It twisted through me, reminding me of another smile, one I missed so much I hurt. "I was about to ask you the same question. Security called and said you were down here. I was heading out, so I thought I'd come by and see if I could point you in the right direction first." He held out his hand for me to shake through the window. "Basil Romano. You must be Wren Heath."

"That's me." His hand was as warm and reassuring as his smile. "Romano . . . as in . . ."

He opened the truck door. "My name is on the company, but my sons made Romano Superstores what it is today. Me, I was happy with one store and a much simpler life. Now why don't I show you the system we'd like you to inspect."

I grabbed my tablet and hopped out of the truck. He closed the door behind me with old-world chivalry. "Thank you," I said.

As we walked, he asked, "So, an engineer, that's impressive—"

"For a woman?" I finished for him in an unusually bold manner. Technically, I'd already quit this job, if only in my head, so I wasn't concerned about saying what I normally would have held back. In my business, I often ran into men who were surprised I had an engineering degree.

"For anyone," he added smoothly. "My wife stayed home with the children, but I would have supported her if she'd chosen to work instead. My oldest son married a brilliant accountant. My boys have excellent taste in women."

His strange compliment made me a little uncomfortable. I cleared my throat. "So the system is in the main building?" I was already there. I might as well finish this last job before quitting.

"Yes." He checked his watch. "And you're here just in time."

"We do try to make the window of time we schedule."

The security guard gave Mr. Romano a thumbs-up when he saw him. It was strange enough that I almost didn't enter the door he held open for us. Was I being paranoid, or was something going on?

Another man met us in the foyer. He was twenty or so years younger, just as tall, with dark hair and gray eyes. "Dad, do you really think this is a good idea?"

Mr. Romano scoffed and said to me, "This is my son Sebastian. He doesn't understand how important it is to inspect sprinkler systems on a regular basis. Not everything takes care of itself."

Sebastian? His name cut through me. I remembered Mauricio talking about his brother with the same name. I looked back and forth between the two men.

That would be a crazy coincidence.

Unless Mauricio had orchestrated it.

No. If he wanted to see me again, wouldn't he have answered my text?

I held out my hand to the younger Romano. "Wren Heath."

He shook my hand firmly, then released it. "You look like a normal enough person."

I smiled weakly. "Thanks?" I waved my tablet. "Maybe it's best if I just get to the job at hand."

"He's here, sir," the security guard announced.

I turned to see who *he* was and swayed on my feet when Mauricio and his near double walked into the foyer. My mouth went dry. The room spun. When our eyes met, it took everything in me not to run and throw myself into his arms.

The only thing that stopped me was the anger in his eyes. "What are you doing here, Wren?"

"I—I—"

"No," Mauricio growled. "You don't get to ghost me the way you did, then waltz in here like nothing happened."

"I sent you a text," I defended as I gathered my composure. There was so much I wanted to say, but I didn't know where to start.

He shook his head angrily. "What are you doing here, Wren? Did you discover I'm filthy rich and have a change of heart?"

Each word slammed through me. In shock, I took a step back, then another. Who was this man? He wasn't the Mauricio from Paris.

"That's enough, Mauricio," his father snapped.

Mauricio's face tightened. "Dad, you don't know what's going on here." He took me by the arm. "Wren, you shouldn't have gotten involved with my family. If you want to talk, let's step outside. I do have a question or two for you."

I yanked my arm free from his hold.

For a moment, when I'd first seen him walk through the door, I'd thought he'd arranged to see me again. Sure, it was awkward for that meeting to happen in front of his father and brothers, but a tiny part of me had hoped that meant he wanted me to meet them.

I didn't understand why I was there, how the universe had folded in such an insane way to put me in that moment, but I knew I wanted out of it. "Don't touch me."

"Don't stalk my family."

Sebastian cut in. "Mauricio, there's something you should know."

"Stalk your family?" My voice rose, and I threw my hands up in the air. "Is that what you think I'm doing? You know what? I'm not sorry I left the way I did. Apparently what happens in Paris stays in Paris, because what we had looks batshit crazy anywhere else. Stay away from me."

"That will be easier to do if you don't hang out where I work," he snapped.

"I'm not hanging . . ." I made an angry sound in my throat. "Whatever." I turned back to Mr. Romano. "My boss will schedule someone else to come out. Goodbye."

Head held high, I spun on my heel and walked out of the building. My pace morphed to a near run as I made my way back to my truck. I didn't slow until after I'd peeled out of the parking lot and was speeding down the highway . . . toward anywhere but there.

CHAPTER TWENTY-FIVE

MAURICIO

I'd almost run after her.

I hadn't because . . . partly because I was still angry and partly because I hadn't been ready to see her. I'd still been mentally preparing what to say to her when I texted her back.

Then—bam—she'd been right there in front of me.

"Well, you handled that like a bull in a china shop," my father said dryly.

I shook my head. "She—she—"

"Had no idea you'd be here," Sebastian interjected. "Dad tracked down her name through your friend in Paris. He thought seeing her again might help you get out of your slump."

My attention flew to my father. He shrugged. "I imagined it going much better."

"You think?" Christof added. "I thought she handled the accusation of being a gold digger with a surprising amount of grace. Some women might have belted him."

As the truth sank in, my heart started thudding wildly and my gut twisted painfully. *No. I couldn't be that big of a dick.* "So she was here . . ."

"Because Dad hired the company she works for to inspect the sprinkler system and requested her specifically." Sebastian rubbed his eyebrows as if the idea had given him a headache.

I turned toward the door she'd run through. "I thought—"

"Come on, you weren't thinking," Christof said.

"I wasn't," I said slowly. *Holy shit.* "I've spent the last few days asking myself if anything she said was true." I ran a hand through my hair. I was still trying to wrap my head around what had just happened. My father had contacted my friend in Paris? Gotten Wren's last name that way? "Dad, you called Felix?"

"That's where I started. He told me his ex-girlfriend knew the woman you'd been seeing."

"And he gave you Cecile's number?"

"Oh no, he didn't want me to contact her, but his mother had her number. I had a good talk with Cecile. She now understands how a broken appendage can affect a man's ability to think straight. I don't know what your excuse is, though."

Oh my God.

"So Wren really had no idea she'd see me today."

My father looked to Sebastian. "He's the pretty one, but has he always been this slow? In a minute I'm going to walk away, wait for one of you to slap some sense into him; then and only then will I come back and try this conversation again."

My father's sarcasm was lost on me. I was deep into replaying everything I'd said to Wren and hating myself for handling seeing her again as badly as I had. "I really am an idiot."

Sebastian gave my back a supportive smack. "Perhaps not in all situations, but in this one, yes."

Christof made a pained face. "You really messed up this time."

I nodded; then I frowned. "A heads-up might have helped."

He shrugged and gave me a look that said, "Don't pin your screwup on me."

"You're right; this is on me. What the hell was I thinking?"

We all stood in the foyer, not moving, not speaking. I felt like a complete ass—worse, an ass pimple. Not even someone with an ass fetish liked those.

My father broke the silence. "Is anyone else wondering how long it'll take Mauricio to wake up and go after her?"

Christof shook his head in mock sadness. "At this rate I'll probably marry before him, and I'm not even dating anyone."

"I shouldn't have doubted her. I should have swung her up into my arms and told her I'd missed her." *That's what I should have done.*

"But now you know you need to . . ." my father began, then let his words hang in the air.

"Excuse me," I said as I stepped away. "She might still be in the parking lot. If not—"

"Try calling her," Christof said with a laugh. "Hey, he needs all the help he can get."

I didn't stick around to debate that claim. I couldn't let Wren leave before I apologized.

CHAPTER TWENTY-SIX

WREN

The highway was a blur. Cars zipped around me, some dangerously close, but they didn't matter. All I cared about was getting as far from what had just happened as I could.

I called Cecile. It rang a few times, but she didn't pick up. The only way any of this made sense was if she'd somehow been involved. Unless she'd told Felix my last name.

How else would Basil Romano have found me? I remembered thinking it was odd that Romano Superstores had requested me specifically.

Why had Mauricio's father asked for me?

Had Mauricio mentioned me?

When I'd fantasized about meeting up with Mauricio again, I certainly hadn't pictured how it had gone. Not only had he figuratively slammed a door in my face, he'd also accused me of wanting to be with him for his money. *So, Cecile, this time I won.*

I didn't laugh at my joke because . . . well, it wasn't funny.

What a fool I'd been.

My phone rang. "Hey, you." It was Cecile.

"Hi," I said with a voice thick with emotion. "Do you have a minute?"

"Of course. What's up?"

Without stopping for a breath, I vomited up what had just happened with Mauricio. Everything from what I'd thought when I first saw him to what I'd said before I'd bolted for the door.

"Oh no," she said with real dismay. "That's not how it was supposed to go."

"What do you mean?"

"Basil called me. It was an enlightening conversation. You're never going to believe what was actually wrong with Felix—a penile fracture."

"Ouch." I remembered joking about it and felt a little guilty. "Not from a car door, I hope."

She chuckled. "No. Nothing quite so dramatic. Funny thing is, once he told me, I wasn't upset with him anymore. It was with some woman he didn't care about. Stupid, but not unforgivable. We've had dinner together since then. Not me and Basil—Felix. Almost losing his manhood has been good for him. It's given him time to think about what he wants his life to look like—businesswise and his personal life. We're going to try things again . . . slowly this time . . . and without seeing other people."

"That's . . . good, I guess? I don't mean to make this about me, but why did you tell Mauricio's father my name and where I worked?"

"He said Mauricio was missing you. His plan to put the two of you in the same place again sounded really romantic. I'm sorry. I didn't consider that it might go badly." Sounding a little defensive, she added, "Plus you wouldn't have been so surprised if you answered my calls. I did try to contact you."

I'd seen two missed calls from Cecile, and I'd meant to call her back. I'd told myself I would after the funeral. Then I'd needed a break before wanting to tell anyone what had happened. "Sorry, things kind of imploded here. I'll tell you about it later. That was kind of sweet of Mauricio's father to set up a meeting for us, but I guess he doesn't know his son as well as he thinks he does, because Mauricio made how he feels about me crystal clear. You were right about him. He's a player. In Paris

Mauricio was who I wanted him to be. But that wasn't real. I'm not going to freak out, though. I can be sad about what our time together wasn't or be glad for the good time we did have."

"Sounds like a healthy way to handle it . . . also feels a little too fast to not be bullshit."

"What do you want me to say? That I'm hurt, embarrassed, angry?"

"Yes. It's true, isn't it?"

I let out a calming breath. "What's the benefit to being angry about something I can't change?"

"No benefit, but it feels good." When I didn't say anything, she added, "You can't bottle everything up. If you're angry, be angry. Yell. Scream. Let it out. I called your mother when I didn't hear back from you, and she told me what happened with your dad. You didn't need this on top of that. Pull over and kick the shit out of a tree. Wait, no, don't break your foot. Let me see if I can find one of those places where you pay to break their dishes."

"Thanks, but I've got this." Just listening to Cecile was making me feel a little better. I wasn't surprised she'd called my mother since I'd recently suggested that as a viable solution. "Do I want to know how Felix fractured his penis?"

"The usual way. The idiot was having sex in a closet at the office."

"Are you sure you want to give him another chance?"

"I gave him a harsh reality check on his behavior, and he took it. Not only was what he did a huge legal no-no, but it's also a bad way to gain the respect of the reigning board. If he doesn't wise up, it won't matter that his father started the company; he won't even be able to get a job in the mail room. I thought he'd be upset by what I said, but he said he appreciated my honesty . . . said he valued my opinion. I like this humble version of him. We didn't talk like this before. We worried more about keeping it light than keeping it real. Who knows, I might even be able to teach him to be better in bed."

I chuckled at that. "I'm sure you can."

"It's all about knowing what you want and going after it, Wren. I didn't realize how much I would miss Felix until we'd broken things off. He says he feels the same way. We'll see."

"I'm happy for you. I think. I don't know. I'm not sure of anything right now. I want to walk into my boss's office today and quit. Does that sound crazy? I've got some money saved, but I feel like if I don't do it today, I never will."

"Do it, then. Break free. Then choose a new path and go after it."

My phone beeped with an incoming call. I glanced down at where the caller ID was displayed on my car's console. Mauricio. Our parting words to each other echoed in my head. The guilt I'd felt had been replaced by anger, but that didn't make me feel any better. I didn't want to carry the weight of his feelings on top of mine. Whatever he had to say, I was certain I didn't want to hear it. I hit "Ignore."

Sorry, the caller you're attempting to contact is breaking free.

CHAPTER TWENTY-SEVEN

DOMINIC

After closing down his office computer, Dominic stood and stretched. The sun was still shining in the sky, but he was done for the day. There'd been a time when work was all he knew, and he'd resented anyone who left work the moment they could. A happy home life had changed his opinion of that. He had enormous responsibilities and holdings in more companies than most people had socks, but he'd learned to delegate as well. Now dinner with his wife and daughter mattered more than if an email had to wait a day to be answered.

No one dared suggest he run his tech empire any other way. He'd fought his way to the top, and the perk of being there was he didn't answer to anyone—except his wife.

He smiled at that thought.

Abby was not above reining him in now and then. He didn't mind at all. Money and power didn't impress her. Kindness, character, and honesty mattered most to her. He hated to imagine who he might have become had she not come into his life.

He was packing up a briefcase to take home when his phone rang. "I'm out the door, Jeremy. What do you need?"

"Do you remember saying you didn't want to know if Alethea had found some of your family?"

"Yes. I believe I was clear about that."

"And I respect your wishes. I gave your daughter the names you gave me, but she's determined to find more about your side of the family. The more she hears the word *no*, the more determined she becomes. Does that sound like anyone you know?"

Dominic frowned. It certainly did.

Jeremy continued, "Have you considered simply telling her what you know? I realize your father wasn't a nice man—"

"Not nice? Not nice? He was a sick human being. Even if he was sorry in the end, the world became a better place the day he died."

"Okay, so maybe don't be that honest with Judy. There must be something you could tell her . . . something about your mother's family?"

"They've never wanted anything to do with me. I won't have them reject my daughter as well."

"So you know them. Are they—?"

"Oh, I know them. At least some of them. They hated my father so much that—" He stopped and continued in his thoughts: *So much that they hid my mother from him. From all of us.*

After his father's death, his mother had resurfaced. Thomas Brogos, the longtime Corisi family lawyer, had brought her to Isola Santos for one fucked-up family reunion. The story his mother had told still sounded unbelievable. Fearing that her husband, Antonio Corisi, would kill her . . . his mother had run back to Montalcino, her hometown. There she'd changed her name and hidden from the wrath of her husband. Not an easy desertion to forgive.

Especially since she'd left her two children behind—in the care of the man she feared.

When she'd first disappeared, Dominic had refused to believe she would have left them voluntarily. He'd searched for her for years. Even had gone to her hometown himself. He'd begged his cousins for any information. Was she alive? Dead? Anything.

They'd given him nothing.

Not then—not since.

After her return, his mother had suggested he visit there with her to meet his cousins, but they would never be more to him than indifferent strangers who had refused to help a desperate young man. "They're dead to me," he finished.

Jeremy cleared his throat. "A lot of time has passed. Things might be different now."

"I don't need more family."

With a sigh, Jeremy said, "Maybe not, but your daughter seems to think you do. She's not dropping this. My opinion, you need to get ahead of this. With or without you, she'll get their names. DNA testing is just a mouth swab and a stamp away. Do you really want her to contact your family there before you do?"

"No, I do not." Dominic ran a hand through his hair in frustration. Judy handled the word *no* as well as he did—which was not well at all. Jeremy was right. She wouldn't stop until she found something. "I know my grandmother's name, but that's all. My mother had a sister, but she doesn't talk about her. Cam . . . Camile? Carmella? I don't remember. I never met either of them. For all I know, my grandmother is dead too."

"Do you—do you want me to go and scope it out for you?"

"No, if I go, I'll go myself. Thanks for the update, Jeremy. I'll handle this from here on out."

CHAPTER TWENTY-EIGHT

MAURICIO

Sunday dinners were normally full of laughter and light ribbing. It was a day we gathered, ate far too many carbs, and caught up on each other's lives. Gian had yet to miss one even though he was living at college.

Usually it was my favorite day of the week. Adding little Ava to the mix put another layer of amusement in the group. She was a lively little girl, very opinionated, and she fit in perfectly. So it was not surprising that she was the first to mention what none of us were willing to call attention to.

"Mommy," Ava said, "why is everyone angry?"

"No one is angry, Ava," her mother reassured her. "It's just been a long week. When people are tired, they don't talk as much."

They were both right and both wrong. My brothers and I were not fighting, but we were off. My father and I were not angry with each other. We had hit a wall, though.

Dad and I had not spoken since he'd ambushed me with Wren.

Sebastian was respectfully trying to stay neutral on the subject.

Christof had finally realized I wasn't laughing at any of his jokes about how I'd fucked up with Wren.

And Gian—no one had updated him yet about what had gone down.

If my mother knew, she wasn't giving a hint of it. Thankfully.

I'd called Wren since not finding her in the parking lot. I didn't leave a message, because what I had to say was too complicated to leave in one. I was still disappointed how she'd simply left Paris, but seeing her again had proved something to me . . . I hadn't imagined how I'd felt about her. She was worth working this through.

I'd texted: I'm sorry too.

Arguably the lamest post-accusation apology.

Not shocking that she had yet to respond to it.

The last thing I wanted to do at Sunday dinner was rehash how I'd messed up. So we ate in relative silence, keeping the conversation mostly on Gian and how his classes were going.

We had just finished the most tender lamb stew when my mother asked if we wanted dessert. Ava was the only one who perked up at the mention. The rest of us looked as ready as I felt for the meal to end.

"I'm going to head out early, Mom," I said, rising to my feet.

Christof stood as well. "Me too. I have meetings to prepare for."

Sebastian rose and nodded to Heather. "We should probably get Ava home early as well."

Mom leaned over and winked at her grandchild. "Ava, you're a smart little girl. Something is going on with my boys. What do you think I should do after they clear the table?"

In a serious tone, she said, "My teachers make us sit at a table and talk."

Mom looked us over and said firmly, "Let's do that now. Everyone sit down."

We all sat.

She went over to where Ava was. "This might be an adult conversation. Do you think you and Wolfie could go play right there in the other room where we can see you? I'm sure everyone will want dessert after I talk to them. Would you like cookies or cake?"

"Cake, please," Ava said, picking up her stuffed animal from the chair beside her. "Can Wolfie and I play with Legos?"

"Absolutely. I'll put them out for you."

My mother and Ava walked away from the table.

I met my father's gaze. "Mom doesn't know?"

Gian asked, "Doesn't know what?"

My father made a face that could have been interpreted either way.

My mother was back before we had time for anything more. She stood there, hands on hips, and said, "Okay, who wants to start?"

Heather stood. "I should join Ava."

"Sit," my mother said.

Eyes wide, Heather retook her seat. My mother loved her like a daughter—well, this was the flip side to that honor.

None of us wanted to be the first to spill. Not even my normally brave father.

After a few minutes of awkward silence, she folded her arms across her chest and turned to her husband. "Who wants to go first?"

"I got involved in something I shouldn't have." He cleared his throat. "I apologize, Mauricio."

My mother's eyebrow arched. "Mauricio?"

I nodded. This needed to be addressed before we could move on. "I'm not upset with you, Dad. I'm disappointed in myself and how I behaved that day."

In a gruff tone, Sebastian added, "I should have given you a heads-up, Mauricio. You shouldn't have walked into that blind."

Christof sighed. "I could have said something as well."

Sounding a little put out, Gian asked, "Why do I have no idea what we're talking about?"

My mother's tone sharpened as she said, "Don't worry, Gian, this has nothing to do with you being away for school. Your father thought I didn't know, and although I see some of your brothers every day, they didn't tell me anything either."

With a smile similar to the smooth one I employed when things were tense, my father said, "Remember how Mauricio fell in love in Paris . . ."

I instantly began to correct that claim. "I wouldn't go as far as—" Then I stopped, because there was no use denying what was painfully obvious.

"Her name is Wren Heath," Christof said. "You'd like her, Heather. She's an engineer. Probably too smart for Mauricio anyway."

I almost told him to shut the fuck up, but respectfully held my tongue in front of our mother. "I've been in a bit of a funk since returning home. I know Dad told all of you that Wren and I were figuring things out. That wasn't entirely true. She ended things with me. I was figuring out how to deal with that, and I understand why Dad did what he did. If I weren't a complete ass—assuming jerk, it might have turned out differently."

"I'm still lost," Gian said.

Mom turned to Dad and pinned him down with a forceful stare. "That's where you thought you would help."

He cracked. "I tracked down Wren to a company based in Connecticut. She lives so close. How could they not be meant to be? I arranged for her to be at our headquarters when Mauricio was there. I hoped a little nudge would get them back on track."

I fisted a hand on the table. "But I messed up royally. I was still angry with her. So when I saw her, I said stupid sh—stuff I didn't mean. Now she's back to not answering my calls."

Mom's lips pursed. She walked over and put a hand on my shoulder. "If love were easy, son, everyone would be with someone."

I wasn't sure how to take that. Was she confirming what I'd always thought about myself? That I wasn't the type for a relationship? Wren had shattered that belief. I'd imagined forever with her, and that was a hard image to unsee. But was I wrong to hold on to it?

After walking back to sit beside my father, my mother asked, "Have you apologized, Mauricio?"

I sat back in my chair and groaned. "I told her to stop stalking my family and implied she was only seeking me out now because she found out I have money. I'm sure she doesn't want to hear from me again."

Sebastian winced and shared a look with Heather.

Christof said to Gian, "It was painful to watch. Almost funny, if he didn't like her so much."

I ran a hand through my hair. "I screwed up what was probably my last chance with her."

Gian looked around the table. "That's depressing." He cocked his head to the side. "Mauricio, what happened to you? I thought you were the guy who could walk into a room and leave with any woman you wanted?"

"I told you, this one is *smart*," Christof interjected with a grin.

I raised one finger in warning toward him, met my mother's gaze, and lowered it. "Christof is right. Wren isn't like anyone I've ever known. She's not only very intelligent, but she is also very close to her family. She's hilarious, especially when she isn't trying to be. And so hot—hotheaded when she cares about a topic. I imagined her here with us . . . She's special. Presently, though, she doesn't have the best impression of me."

Heather chuckled and took Sebastian's hand in hers. "That is sometimes the case with Romano men. Sebastian didn't give up, though. And I'm glad he didn't." She met my gaze. "If you show Wren this side of you, she'll forgive your first stumbles."

Of everyone I knew, the opinions of these people mattered the most to me. "I'm not good at this romance stuff. I'm used to women chasing me."

Christof coughed and said, "The sad thing is, he's being sincere, Heather. I've never seen a woman turn him down."

"What does that say about your choice of companionship prior to Wren, Mauricio?" Mom asked in light reprimand.

It wasn't a question I hadn't asked myself, so I had a quick answer. "That I wasn't ready for anything serious before now."

She smiled.

My father nodded in approval.

"My impression of her family is that they are hardworking, good people who raised their daughter to be smart enough to want more than you've offered her so far."

My jaw dropped. "Mom, how do you have any impression at all of her family?"

"I met her mother for lunch. Very nice woman."

"You did what?" Was I going insane, or was the rest of the world? "When? How?"

My mother poured herself a cup of coffee. "How? Your father thinks I can't hear him when he's in the other room, but since his hearing started to go, I can't not know what he's saying on the phone. I felt horrible that I didn't step in from the beginning, but . . ." She placed her hand over my father's. "It was so romantic it reminded me of when we were dating. I wanted your plan to work."

My father leaned over and kissed her cheek. "Me too. Thank you for having faith in me."

"Always," she assured him.

I broke in. "Can we get back to you having lunch with Wren's mother? What did you tell her? What did she tell you? Is Wren okay?"

My mother sighed. "Wren is going through a tough time, Mauricio. Her mother and I had a long talk, and Wren had a good reason to leave Paris the way she did."

"Is it . . ." I hated to even ask. "Is it someone else?"

"No, but I think it's best if she tells you the rest herself. What I can say is that she has a lot going on in her life right now. She could use a good friend . . . and more if that's where you're meant to go together. But Mauricio, before you contact her again, are you sure? I don't want to see her hurt."

I took a moment to let it all wash over me. Whatever Wren was facing, I wanted to be there for her. I *would* be there for her.

Some would be angry with their parents for getting involved at all, but I couldn't be. I wasn't upset with any of my family. If things worked out, they would welcome Wren to the family and love her as if she'd been born one of us. If Wren never spoke to me again, they would still all be there . . . supporting me, pushing me, and sometimes driving me crazy until I was over her.

I didn't want to be over her.

I wanted her there, at my parents' table, laughing with me each time my mother brought us all to heel. I could picture her doing the same with the children we'd have.

I tried to imagine how the meeting had gone between our mothers and couldn't. "Wren said her mother can change a flat tire. Wren is strong and independent. Is that how her mother came across?"

My mother nodded. "And down to earth. She's faced some tough times, too, but is now where she wants to be." She looked across the table at me. "She wants her daughter to find a nice man to settle down with. Someone who will help her reach her dreams instead of holding her back. I told her you could be that man."

Not could be. "I am that man."

Behind his hand, Gian said, "So it seems like the only hurdle is that she won't answer your calls, Mauricio. Might be time to go old school and do this in person."

"Old school," I repeated with amusement. How had face-to-face become novel and retro? He was right, though. It was time to change my approach. "That sounds like a plan."

"Just don't buy her father a cow," my mother joked.

My dad leaned forward and said, "The cow worked. Don't underestimate the power of the cow."

"He's speaking figuratively, right?" Christof asked.

"No," my mother said with a laugh. "He literally bought a cow for my father when we were dating."

My father wiggled his eyebrows at me. "And I was always her father's favorite."

"Who wants dessert?" my mother asked.

We all said we did. My father and I offered to retrieve it from the kitchen. Once we were alone my father said, "I am sorry, son. I wanted to make things better."

"You did, Dad. I'm taking your advice this time. I've been impatient and more concerned with how I felt than why she left the way she did. I'm going to take it slower this time." I gave him a quick hug. "And if her father needs a 'cow,' I'll figure out how to get one for him."

A huge smile spread across my father's face; then he said, "It doesn't actually have to be a cow. You get that, right?"

I picked up a stack of plates and handed him the cake. "Yeah, Dad. Don't worry. I got this."

To lighten the mood, when I placed the plates on the table, I said, "Now for the important question. Mom, did Wren's mother say if she can cook?"

Laughter accompanied a few groans. Ava walked back into the room. "Cake!"

I swung her up into my arms and spun with her. "Finally, someone who shares my priorities."

Giggling, she hugged me back. Then very seriously she said, "I don't want to share my cake."

Laughter erupted again, and just like that we were back.

CHAPTER TWENTY-NINE

WREN

Monday afternoon, I was on my couch with my laptop, hunting through online job listings. When I'd quit my job, I'd offered my boss two weeks' notice, and he'd offered me a more immediate termination. So I'd gotten what I'd wanted—instant unemployment.

Whee.

So far breaking free was terrifying.

Like stepping off into an abyss and free-falling into the unknown.

I shrugged, trying to release the tension. Change was supposed to be scary, wasn't it? This was me taking charge of my life and reshaping it.

Part of me wanted to claim temporary insanity and beg for my old job back.

I refused to give in to that weakness.

So far I'd updated my résumé and had at least familiarized myself with what a wide variety of companies were looking for. All I had to decide was what I wanted to do with the rest of my life.

That's all.

Easy.

The ringing of my phone was a welcome reprieve. "Hello?"

It was Cecile. "I have a hypothetical question for you."

"Ooookay."

"Let's say Mauricio Romano contacted me and asked me where he could find you. Would you want me to tell him where you are?"

I nearly dropped my laptop. "He called you?"

"I have him on hold. What do you want me to say?"

"Why does he want to see me again? I told you what he said to me the last time. He told me to stay away from him and his family. Does he think I need another warning? I haven't so much as said his name since that day."

"I can merge him into the conversation."

"No." I put my laptop aside and stood. "I don't understand this, Cecile."

"I don't either, but considering my current level of involvement . . . if things work out between you two, I want special treatment at the wedding. What's a higher status than maid of honor?"

Panic swirled through me. I wasn't ready for her jokes. "Cecile, this is serious. What do you think he wants?"

"Hang on."

I was not only freaking out, pacing my apartment, but now I was also on hold. I told myself to breathe. Relax.

This doesn't mean anything.

You only get hurt when you start to second-guess what is happening. He said he was sorry. He probably just wants to apologize.

Cecile came back on. "He wants to see you. In person. Today if you're available."

"I'm not," I said in a rush. "I have . . . I have . . . Cecile, I made myself okay with never seeing him again."

"So . . . tomorrow?" she asked in a tone laced with humor.

"I'm not even showered. And he couldn't come here. What if he just wants sex? I was okay with that in Paris, but now that I'm home I can't—"

"You know what, I'm just going to tell him you're home now and you two can work it out." With that, she hung up.

And I did my best to keep breathing. Cecile didn't joke about stuff like that.

I texted Mauricio: I'm not dressed.

Then groaned and added: I'm not naked, just still in my pajamas.

Still feeling I had to clarify, I wrote: Not sexy ones. Big, baggy old ones.

I could almost hear his amused tone when I read his answer: I love it when you talk dirty to me.

I frowned as I remembered what he'd said the last time I'd seen him. I responded: They're my favorite pair. They're the kind of pajamas a woman who is only interested in a man once she knows he has money wears.

My emotions were all over the place. I was still angry with him, still telling myself I was over him, but knowing that he wanted to see me again filled me with an anticipation I couldn't deny. Every moment we'd shared, every touch, every kiss, every laugh was still so vivid. Of course it was tempting to want another taste of that, but I reminded myself that it wasn't real. Fantasy was fine in Paris.

But here? He would only be a distraction that would stop me from finding that job I want . . . or from being there for Dad.

Sorry, Mauricio, I've already closed the door on what we had.

His response took a moment to come in: I'm in a pair of jeans and T-shirt. It's what most men wear after they've said something incredibly stupid to a woman and are hoping she'll give them another chance.

My hands shook as I read the message over.

Another chance.

It was easy to say I didn't want one when I wasn't sure he was actually interested in one. I wasn't ready to open myself to all the confusion that came along with how I felt about him. You embarrassed and hurt me.

I know. I'm sorry. I was still angry that you left the way you did. That's not an excuse—just the truth.

I'd almost forgotten that he didn't know why I'd left. My reasons didn't belong in that conversation, but it did make me more understanding of his reaction to seeing me again.

I had reasons I needed to come home early and I wasn't ready to share them.

With me.

Yes.

How about now?

Now? Right now?

I can be there in fifteen minutes. I live a few towns over. We'll go somewhere crazy public if you want or just sit on the steps of your building. I don't want to call or text you. I want to see you—face to face.

Right now.

The idea of saying no to him fell away beneath the weight of how much I'd missed him. He'd claimed enough of a piece of my heart that his absence was harder to bear than the uncertainty that came along with seeing him again.

I need time to shower.

If I remember—that's about an hour. Hold on, without me, things might go faster. Thirty minutes?

What a ballbuster he was. I liked it . . . had missed that as well. Thirty minutes. I'll meet you on the street outside my apartment building. You have the address?

I do. All I owe Cecile is a kidney. We don't need both, though, right?

Funny, but I was now on the clock. See you in a few.

I tossed my phone on my bed as I flew past it to the bathroom. It did indeed go faster without him, but as I soaped down I closed my eyes and gave myself over to the memory of his hands lathering me up. His mouth. The crazy position we tried and how proud I'd been of myself for being able to orgasm and maintain my balance at the same time. Not an easy feat.

My body was humming and ready for Mauricio.

My mind was in quite a different place.

I needed someone I could depend on . . . someone who would understand how important my parents were to me. Mauricio was a player. A good time. Seeing him again would only be an exercise in frustration.

For both of us.

I wasn't the woman he thought I was. Maybe he needed to see that.

I switched the water to cold long enough to snap myself back to the task at hand, then rushed through washing and rinsing my hair. Nearly slipped and fell in my haste to wrap a towel around myself and locate my hair dryer at the same time.

A few minutes later, dry and styled, I stood frozen in front of my closet.

I'd been in jeans the last time Mauricio had seen me.

He said he loves a good dress.

He also said he prefers me naked, and that isn't happening either.

I grabbed a pair of jeans, a T-shirt, and an older pair of undies and bra. If I could have instantly grown a week of leg hair, I would have done that as well.

Nothing is going to happen today. We're going to talk. That's it.

Two people meeting one last time, realizing that what they'd had wasn't meant to be long term.

I applied a light amount of makeup . . . enough to give me confidence but not enough to look like I was trying to impress him. I would not be one of those women who threw themselves at his . . . midsection.

I gave myself a stern look in the mirror.

I'm a strong, intelligent, grown woman. I can handle meeting up with an ex-lover. People do it all the time. They're mature enough to understand that not every relationship has to be forever. He wants to know why I left. Does he even deserve an explanation? It didn't take much for him to think the worst of me.

The problem is I want to see him again.

Kiss him.

Wrap myself around him like a love-crazed anaconda.

No, that's not what I want—not what I'll allow myself to want. This is about proving to myself that we have nothing in common and no need to see each other again.

It was impossible to ignore the warm pink of my cheeks. There was excitement in my eyes, and I felt as nervous as a teen heading out on their first date. There was no denying that I still wanted Mauricio.

But it was not going to happen.

Shit, right now. He's probably already waiting for me.

I narrowed my eyes and wagged a finger at my reflection.

No sex.

CHAPTER THIRTY

MAURICIO

No sex.

I muttered that affirmation while leaning on my car in front of Wren's apartment building. It was a battle to not ring her bell, ask to be let upstairs, and see if the chemistry we'd had in Paris would be just as explosive in Danbury, Connecticut.

But that was the mistake I made the last time. I rushed when I should have taken more time to get to know her. This time, I'm doing it right.

It didn't help that my cock was already stiff and swollen. I couldn't blame the guy. He was excited to see her too.

But he'll have to share some of my blood supply, because I need to be able to form full, coherent, persuasive sentences.

I directed my next warning to my dick. *Work with me, or you'll never see her again either.*

Wren stepped through the outer door of her building. The sun lit her blonde hair, and when she smiled at me, I was struck again by the beauty of her. Inside and out. I forced myself to not close the distance between us and haul her in for a kiss.

First we talk.

I reminded myself about what my mother had said. Wren was going through something, and as much as I wanted her, I also wanted to be the friend she needed. I smiled as I remembered my mother had overheard my father's plan to hire Wren's inspection company so we could meet. She'd known, but she'd let him go forward with it because she trusted him the same way the rest of us did. She wanted him to succeed. They were true partners, friends first . . . everything else was frosting.

I'd had the frosting before the cake.

I wanted more. I wanted Wren to hear me planning something anyone else would have thought was crazy and for her to trust me because we were that solid.

Her cheeks flushed as she approached.

I pushed off the car and employed maximum control over myself when I bent and kissed her on the cheek. "You look amazing," I said.

She blinked a few times. "You do too." Then she closed her eyes briefly as if regretting what she'd said.

"I know," I said as I flexed for her. She laughed just as I knew she would.

We stood there for a moment, simply looking at each other. Eventually, she said, "It's beautiful out today. We could take a walk."

"I'd like that." It was a semiresidential neighborhood. Enough traffic so children wouldn't be playing in the streets, but enough private homes with large yards scattered around that, if it weren't the middle of the day, I could imagine being full of families. Safe. Middle class. "Have you lived here long?"

Her hand accidentally brushed against mine. Heat shot through me. I could have taken her hand then, but I was determined to go slowly.

"A few years. I found the place after college. Although I wanted to stay close to my parents, I wanted my own place. They live one town over."

I smiled. "I made the same decision after college. You and I have a lot in common."

She searched my face before turning her attention back to the sidewalk. "You always say the right thing."

Normally that would have sounded more like a compliment. "Not always."

She gave me that look again—the one that made my heart sink a little. "Either way, Paris was amazing. I'm sorry I left the way I did. My father . . ." Her voice trailed off.

I waited.

I didn't want more than she was ready for.

This time, patience would be my first, middle, and last name.

Wren was worth it.

She started again. "My father struggles with PTSD. He lost his arm along with several of his friends to an IED while serving in the Gulf. He's never been the same since. Physically he's fine, but he carries a lot of guilt, and while I was in Paris with you, one of his closest friends died. Trev had been there that day. He understood the demons that haunt my father. When no one else could, Trev could talk him back from the darkness of it."

Her eyes began to glisten with tears, and I could barely breathe. Still, I forced myself to simply nod and listen.

"I spoke to my mother the morning I left. My father went out the night before, right after receiving the call about Trev. He hadn't taken his cell phone with him, and she had no idea where he was. I didn't know what to do."

I almost said she should have woken me. I would have helped her, but something told me that wasn't what she needed in that moment. Instead I reached out, laced my fingers with hers, and said, "So you flew home. I would have done the same."

Her hand tightened on mine. "When I left the note, I wasn't thinking about how you would feel. I wasn't thinking about how I felt. I just had to find my dad."

"You did the right thing, Wren." I stopped and pulled her into my arms. Yes, there was heat, but that moment was more about comforting her. I breathed her in. She sighed and relaxed against my chest.

When she raised her head, I released her. She sniffed and dabbed at the corners of her eyes. "I did. He's still struggling with the loss of Trev, but he's home, and he's talking to someone now at the VA."

I didn't think it was possible to care more for Wren than I did, but I was humbled by the love and loyalty she had for her family. I smiled. "And there I was thinking it was all about me. I was a real ass when I saw you the other day. I fell for you hard in Paris and I was . . . angry . . . hurt, I guess, when I thought you'd seen our time together as much less."

Her eyes riveted to mine. "You were hurt by my note?"

I shrugged. "Is it so hard to believe I have feelings?"

She shook her head slowly. "What are you doing?"

"What do you mean? I'm being honest with you."

She clasped her hands in front of her.

"I've been an idiot." I lifted and dropped a shoulder. "It's why I took it so hard when you left. No one had ever made me feel the way you did. I started imagining forever—"

"No. You told me you don't do relationships. You said if I was looking for forever, it wouldn't be with you."

"I said a lot of things I'm not proud of. It took you leaving to—"

"Stop." She blinked a few times fast again. "I'm home, Mauricio. What worked in Paris doesn't work here. I'm not going to hop right back into bed with you. I just left my job. My dad is good, but I don't know how long that will last. I have responsibilities. I'm sorry."

"What are you saying?"

"I'm saying I don't want to see you again. I met you today because I didn't want to leave things the way they were. I'm not looking for a fling. I need something more substantial with a man who is based in reality—not fantasy."

I held her hand to my chest. "I'm real."

She pulled her hand free. "We're too different."

"You don't know that."

She rolled her eyes and waved a hand at me. "Look at you. Look at me. Your family is rich. My dad owns a gas station, and my mother was a maid. *I'm* currently unemployed. So tell me, how are we similar?"

I frowned. How could she not see that none of that mattered?

A thought occurred to me that brought a smile back to my face. The reason why Wren couldn't see herself with me was because she'd only seen the Paris side of me. The younger me had needed the flash of the city or the thrill of the wild life. That hadn't been me in a long time.

Something my brother's wife had said came back to me then: "If you show Wren this side of you, she'll forgive your first stumbles."

I took her hand back in mine and gave it a squeeze. "Come to dinner with my family on Sunday. If you are not absolutely in love with me by the time you leave, I'll never bother you again."

Her eyes widened. "Dinner?"

A grin spread across my face. She looked so intimidated by the idea I decided to lighten the mood a little. "Don't worry, I'm not Cecile. A Romano dinner starts with antipasti, then several more courses, lots of laughter, and a homemade dessert. Paris was fun, but that's not all of who I am either. Before you write us off, don't you think you should at least meet the real me?"

"I suppose." She looked a little shell-shocked by the idea, so I guided her back to her building. I could have stayed, but I didn't want to give her time to start overthinking my request.

"I'll pick you up at three on Sunday afternoon. Dress casual and come hungry."

I gave her a quick kiss, spun on my heel, and walked away. Once inside my car, I glanced back and saw her standing there, hand on her mouth, still looking like she didn't understand what had just happened.

That was okay. I wasn't sure I did either. I couldn't justify my confidence that this would all work out.

I just knew it would.

As I drove away, I called my mother. "Mom, set another plate out on Sunday. I'm bringing Wren home to meet the family."

She called my father over so he could hear me say those words again.

I gave them a summary of how I'd gone for a walk with her and decided it was time for her to see there was more to me. "She said yes, so I left before she could change her mind."

My father laughed. "Wise man. Less is more."

"Call her tonight," my mother said.

"You don't think that's too much?" I asked.

"Not considering what she's gone through lately. You won't win her heart with smooth words or even the grand gesture of bringing her here. I'm proud of the caring man you've become. When Sebastian needed you, you were there for him. When he didn't need you as much, you stepped back to give him room. You've got a good heart, Mauricio, and people often overlook that because you were blessed with a pretty face. Call her. Ask her about her day. Cheer her on if she needs it. The reason people like you is because you care about them. Show her that side as well."

"Ditto on everything your mother said," my father chimed in.

Gratitude made it difficult to speak for a moment. "Thanks, Mom. Thanks, Dad. You're right, I'm pretty great." I added the last part just to make them laugh.

They did.

Before hanging up, my mother joked, "No pressure, but I have five future grandchildren riding on this." Proving once again that Dad had told her everything.

Although I hoped not *everything*.

I remembered once asking Wren, "What am I going to do with you?"

Her response had been a breathtaking, "Something so decadent I fly home smiling."

She hadn't left Paris the way we'd both hoped she would, but rather than lament how our first time together had ended, I would make it my mission to give her endless reasons to smile—in and out of bed.

I'd been a wild one.

Those days were gone.

I finally knew what I wanted to do, and every part of my plan involved convincing Wren that we belonged together.

CHAPTER THIRTY-ONE

WREN

The week went by in a blur. I sent out résumés during the day, did some phone interviews, and visited my parents daily. This time it wasn't because I was worried about them but because seeing them calmed me.

Surprisingly enough, so did talking to Mauricio every night. When he'd called the evening of our walk, I'd thought he was going to suggest meeting up before Sunday. He didn't. Instead he asked me how my job hunt was going and had seemed genuinely interested as I described each position I was considering applying for.

He'd even offered to look over my résumé and give me feedback on it. With his encouragement, I added more information about awards I had won in college. I'd almost forgotten about them until he'd asked me what achievement had brought me the most pride.

Sad that I'd had to reach back to college for one, but remembering that time in my life convinced me to cross off several of the jobs I'd considered on my list. I hadn't quit one unchallenging, safe job to exchange it for another.

Talking on the phone removed the physical distraction of our attraction. I discovered that Mauricio was pretty sharp when it came to business. He saw trends, understood how to build a customer base, and wasn't afraid to take a risk.

By midweek we had also discussed the crossroads he found himself at. He and his brothers had built Romano Superstores. He knew the business inside and out. Staying made sense, but now it was time for him to step down and let Sebastian take the lead for good.

A warmth filled his voice every time he spoke about his family. My impression of him as cocky and self-absorbed was replaced by the revelation that he had a different side to him—one that was all about his family and his commitment to them.

In Paris we'd spent a lot of time joking around and flirting. This was different, a deeper level of understanding each other. He said he wanted to be with me, not just in my bed, and slowly, with each conversation, I was beginning to want the same thing.

By the end of the week, I was texting him photos of sketches I'd done over the years of inventions I thought the world needed. Some were silly. A lot of people walked into their houses and placed their shoes on mats or tossed them in a pile because they didn't want to track dirt into their homes. I had an idea for a floor mat shoe sanitizer that stopped the need for people to ask their friends to remove their shoes.

He'd said he was impressed, that it should have been already on the market. I'd accepted the compliment, because I'd always been proud of that design.

I'd clarified, though, that shoe sanitizing wasn't what I'd call a passion. What I'd enjoyed was the creative side of designing something people might actually use.

When Sunday finally came, I was excited to see Mauricio again. Yet I was nervous that the day included meeting his family, especially after the scene some of them had witnessed between us. Without the phone calls, I might have found a reason not to go. I would have been too uncomfortable.

As I waited for Mauricio to arrive at my apartment, I was looking forward to meeting the people he'd told me so much about. I wanted to talk to the accountant his brother had married. I loved that her daughter was so much a part of their family now.

Mauricio had told me about Gian's attachment issues that stemmed from his mother wanting nothing to do with him. I loved that his family rallied around each other when one of them needed support. That was how my family was.

That was the kind of family I wanted to have for myself.

Was it possible that Mauricio could be the fantasy and the reality?

When he texted that he was downstairs, I took one last look at myself in the mirror. I'd chosen a simple dress with sandals. My hair was tied back. Almost no makeup. I could have done more, but Mauricio said I was about to meet the real him . . . and I wanted to do that as the real me. I'd almost chosen slacks, but the dress was for Mauricio.

And for me—I wanted to see his eyes light up when he saw it.

They did.

On the sidewalk beside his car, he took my hands in his and spun me around. "You look stunning."

He did as well. Simple tan trousers and a white shirt, but somehow on him they looked like they belonged in a clothing catalog. His smile was just for me; it lit his eyes, filled me with a giddy flutter.

I went up onto my tiptoes and gave him a bold kiss.

His arms slid around me.

I melted into him.

There was fire in his touch, promise in his hunger, but there was also more. After a week of talking, being with him again felt—right.

We were both breathing raggedly when we separated.

"You ready?" he asked in a strangled tone.

I nodded.

He opened the door.

I slid in.

He was in the driver's seat a second later, buckling in and smiling. "My family is crazy," he warned.

"Now you tell me," I joked. I wasn't worried. So was mine. "I hope your mother likes me."

After pulling out into traffic, he took my hand in his and brought it to his lips for a kiss. "She will. She already adores your mother."

I tensed. "My mother?"

"They talk every day. You didn't know that?"

"Hang on. Our parents talk every day?"

"Our mothers do. My father thinks I should meet your father before he does. He's old-fashioned like that."

Like a fish out of water, my mouth opened and shut a few times. "You're pulling my leg, right?"

His smile was easy. "Did I not preface this conversation with notice that my family is nuts?"

"I can't believe my mother never said anything." That was the part I was having trouble with.

"She probably didn't want to influence you—wanted you to realize how wonderful I am on your own."

I couldn't let that one slide. I turned toward him. "What's it like to have such a . . . healthy ego?"

My question didn't rock him at all. He flashed me another smile and winked. "Bigger is better, or so the ladies have always told me."

"Too bad they weren't referring to your brain," I tossed back.

I knew by the slant of his smile where his mind was going before he spoke. "Is that what had you calling out my name and begging me not to stop? My *brain*?"

I couldn't help it; I was flushing and smiling back. I tried to think of a really good comeback, then gave up and just laughed. After a moment, I asked, "I still don't believe our mothers have been talking. Did you make that happen?"

"That was all Mom. The good news? If you decide to be with me, my family will welcome you as one of their own. The bad news? They'll treat you as one of their own. Expect a phone call every day, and Sunday dinners are kind of mandatory."

That didn't sound so bad to me. "I like spending time with family. I'm pretty sure my father will threaten your life, but he hasn't actually killed any of the men I've dated." For fun, I added, "Maimed a few, but not in a way they were able to prove in court."

He barked out a laugh. "I look forward to meeting him."

Fingers laced with his, I said aloud, "We're doing this. You're introducing me to your parents."

He kissed my hand again, "Seemed like the right thing to do considering I'm in love with you."

Love.

Holy shit.

He loves me.

I hadn't allowed myself to analyze how he made me feel. Everything about him, from the first moment we'd met, had felt like a dream. I was still free-falling, waiting to wake up.

The past week had been so good, but could anything that good be true?

In the silence that followed, I realized I hadn't said I loved him back.

I hadn't said anything.

Did I love him? I didn't know. I felt giddy and nauseated. Scared and euphoric as I thought about a future with him.

Was that love?

I wanted what he'd said to be true so bad my stomach was churning.

I covered my mouth with one hand. If I threw up in his lap, he might take that as a sign I didn't love him back, and that wasn't the case.

My head was spinning with the realization that I did love him.

My heart burst with joy.

And me? I started hyperventilating again.

CHAPTER THIRTY-TWO

MAURICIO

After I pulled into my parents' driveway, I checked out Wren's face. She had the wild-eyed, panicky look similar to the expression she'd had on the top of the Eiffel Tower. I gave her a reassuring smile. "My parents are going to love you. Nothing to worry about."

"Yeah," she said breathlessly.

"Ready?"

Her throat bobbed; then she grabbed my arm. "I love you too. I should have said it right away. I meant to. I started thinking about it, and then it was too late. But I do. I love you."

"I know." How could I not fall even deeper in love with her? She was adorable.

Her forehead furrowed. "You do?"

I hadn't until she'd said it. I'd hoped. But what mattered in that moment was that she was shaken, and it was tangling her up on the inside. That wasn't how I wanted her to meet my parents. So I gave her my smoothest playboy smile and struck a model pose. "How could you not?"

Her eyes narrowed, then lit with humor, and she relaxed. "I can never tell if you're kidding."

"Play your cards right today, and you'll have all the time in the world to figure it out." That one she had to know was a joke.

"So that's how it is, is it?" Her grin held a challenge.

I grinned right back. "That's how it is."

"What would you do if your parents didn't like me?" she asked, suddenly serious.

It was an important question that deserved an honest answer. "They're not allowed that option."

She searched my face, then said, "You mean that, don't you?"

I kissed her. I couldn't not. Then I murmured, "I do, Kitten."

She shoved me back. "Do not call me that in front of your parents."

I chuckled and rubbed my chest. She was stronger than she looked. "So how do you want me to say we met?"

Her eyes rounded again. "I hadn't thought of that. What did you tell them so far?"

"That we met through a friend."

"That's it?"

"I wasn't sure they could handle your near threesome with Felix."

She raised a finger as she clarified, "I never even considered it."

"Not even when you thought I was him? I saw the way you looked at me."

Her mouth dropped open; then she smiled and conceded. "Okay, just for a second when I saw you. But I don't share."

I grinned back at her. "Good, because I don't either."

She leaned toward the windshield. "Your family is watching us through the windows."

It was difficult to look away from her, but I did. "Yep. My parents are the ones at the door. Sebastian, Heather, and Ava are in the bay window. I think that's Christof behind them. It has to be, because Gian's in the window of the bathroom. I hope he remembers to wash his hands."

"Doesn't he always?"

I shrugged. "I think so. I don't know. He wants to be a doctor, so his hygiene is probably above average. Yeah, I'm going with 'It's not a problem.'"

She gave me a long look, then burst out laughing. "What are you even talking about?" Then she touched my cheek. "Are you nervous?"

I hadn't realized until then that I was. A man only did this once—introduced his future wife to his family. I wanted it to go well. "They're wonderful people, Wren. All the best of me is because of them."

She gave my hand a squeeze. "Then I already love them, because I'm pretty attached to the best of you."

My smile turned wicked. A man can't help where his mind goes.

She rolled her eyes, but she was smiling. "You know that's not what I meant."

As I stepped out of the car, I joked, "Don't be embarrassed. I'm pretty fond of that part of me as well."

"Oh my God," she said with a laugh.

I opened her door and took her hand. "Just go easy on the smut talk in front of my parents."

"Stop," she said, smacking my arm lightly.

"Never," I promised.

My parents waved to us as we approached. As soon as we reached them, my mother enveloped Wren in a hug. My father did the same. When Wren didn't immediately respond by pulling away and running, I knew she'd survive the rest of the evening.

Sebastian met us in the hallway and introduced her to Heather as well as Ava and her stuffed animal. Wren bent down and greeted the stuffed animal with the same warm smile she gave Ava.

Dinner was absolutely delicious. Conversation flowed with ease. My mother had wisely suggested Wren and I sit across from Sebastian and Heather.

The instant comfort level between Heather and Wren made sense. It was easy to see how much Wren admired Heather for having her own business. Heather seemed equally impressed that Wren had chosen a field that was still male dominated.

"If you could do anything, what would you want to be doing?" Heather asked.

Wren had lowered her eyes for a moment, then admitted, "When I allow myself to imagine everything is possible . . . I dream of inventing something that matters and making that my job. They say when you do something you love, it's not work. My father and I used to talk about creating something together when I was old enough to, but that never happened." She lowered her eyes again. "For now, though, it's more important I find something steady. Not having a job is scary to someone like me, so eventually I have to choose something and go with it."

"What do your parents do?" Gian asked with the bold innocence of the young.

I put an arm around the back of Wren's chair. Would she be embarrassed to say it here? My family didn't judge people by the size of their wallet, but she'd already admitted she found our wealth intimidating.

Wren raised her eyes and smiled at Gian, seeming to get that his question stemmed from genuine interest. "My father owns a gas station. He lost an arm in the Gulf War, but before that he was also an engineer . . . so needing to know how things work is what I inherited from him. My mother cleaned houses to bring in extra money. I got my work ethic from her. Food on the table first, then you can chase your dreams. I never wanted for anything when I was younger. So I do what I can now to help them."

I caressed Wren's back. "Wren's very close to her family, but you know that, right, Mom?"

My mother had the grace to blush. "Wren, I suppose it's time I fess up. I've been talking with your mother. She's a lovely woman. I hope I haven't overstepped."

Christof leaned over and stage-whispered, "We all know it's too much. All you can do is accept it. There's no other option."

My mother sat back, looking unusually defensive. "Of course there's another option. You make me sound like I'm not open to criticism."

211

We all remained carefully quiet.

Wren hadn't gotten the memo. She said, "I'll admit that when I heard you'd called her, I thought it was too much."

All the air left the room, as if in a whoosh. I doubt anyone even took a breath.

Wren continued, "But you raised four boys. I don't know how the other three were, but I'm sure this one was a handful." She cocked a thumb at me.

My mother laughed. "He sure was." Our hearts began beating again.

"You love them, and you want the best for them. I respect that. The world is a harsh place, and there is nothing wrong with doing everything you can to keep your babies safe for as long as you can." She leaned forward. "I'd like a big family, and if I'm ever lucky enough to have one, you can bet your life I will want to know who my children spend time with." She turned and smiled up at me. "And I hope my children come out as good as yours have . . ." She pinched the air. "Perhaps a smidge more humble."

There was general laughter in response.

I kissed her, just above her ear, then joked, "They will if they come out ugly like Christof . . ."

Christof winged a bread roll at my head. I saw it coming and ducked in time.

I laughed and added, "Or slow as Gian."

Gian balled up a napkin but missed as well.

"Or as grumpy as Sebastian—"

A meatball hit me smack in the middle of my forehead, but not from Sebastian. As I wiped it off, Ava exclaimed, "Score!"

"That's my girl," Sebastian said with humor. "She's got a pitcher's arm."

Looking like she was holding back laughter, Heather said, "Ava, we don't throw food."

Ava looked around the table and argued, "They do."

My mother gave each of us a stern look. "Not at my table, they don't."

"Sorry, Mom," my brothers and I said in unison.

My mother's expression relaxed, and she turned to Wren again. "Take a good look, Wren. This is us on our best behavior. You think you can handle it?"

Wren looked around the table as if giving the question real consideration. I tensed beside her. She wasn't one to dance around what she thought, and my mother had just put her on the spot.

Love and hope met me when Wren looked into my eyes and said, "I know I can. I prefer a little messiness to anything that's too perfect."

My family faded to the background for a moment, and I joked, "Are you calling my family messy?"

With a grin, she wiped a napkin across my forehead and turned it to show me how I had missed a bit of sauce. "I am, what are you going to do about it?"

There wasn't much I could do with the audience we had. Still, a man had his pride. "Ava, get a meatball ready."

"Don't," Heather interjected quickly. "He's joking."

I wiggled my eyebrows at Wren. "Am I?"

Wren's eyes sparkled, and her grin widened. "Bring it if you dare."

My father cleared his throat. "Ava, don't let Uncle Mauricio get you in trouble. We've met our food-throwing quota for one evening. How about you and I go see what's for dessert?"

"Yay," Ava exclaimed.

I didn't take my eyes from Wren's. "If battle lines are being drawn, I should warn you I bought Ava a pony. I'm kind of her favorite."

Wren ran a hand over my now-clean forehead. "Unless you tease Sebastian."

I smiled back, loving the ease of the banter between us. "That goes without saying. One day I hope my children toss a meatball in my defense."

She laughed. "Is that what life with you would be like?"

I laced my hand with hers and promised, "That and so much more."

Her expression became serious as well. "This is all so fast. I haven't figured out me yet."

"I'm still a work in progress as well." Bringing her home had been the right choice, though. Where there had been fear before, I saw hope in her eyes. "What if the answer is that we should figure it out together?"

I'd never forget the love I saw in her expression when she said, "I'd like that."

A quick glance around the table confirmed what I'd sensed—my family had cleared their plates and retreated to the kitchen. We were alone. "I love you, Wren. This is the real deal for me. You tell me what you need, and I'll move heaven and earth to make sure you have it."

She closed her eyes. When she opened them, there was love, but also determination. "I'd love to say you're all I need, but that's not the truth. My father relies more on me now than ever before. My heart breaks seeing him teeter, because I don't know if I have what it takes to be his Trev. I'm scared I might fail. He'll love you because I love you, but I can't build any life that doesn't allow me to be his rock."

"I'd never ask you to choose." My heart did a funny little flip.

Her hand tightened on mine. "I know, I just had to be clear. I'm a package deal."

I caressed her cheek gently. "I understand that. I am as well. Family obligations don't scare me. I love that you are stepping up to help your father . . . especially when you're trying to find your own way . . ." A thought hit me like a kick to the head. "Do you trust me?"

Her eyes widened slightly but she nodded.

"I don't mean about something little. I mean about something big—something that if I made it happen might be the answer to what you're looking for."

"With my job?"

"With everything."

"That's a big something."

"Yes, but the more I think about it, the more I know it's what we both need."

Her forehead furrowed. "Want to let me in on it?"

Looking down into her eyes, I said, "Let me get the groundwork done for it. I'm excited about this." I gripped both of her hands in mine. "I want to do this for you, Wren—for us. Once I have the details sorted out, I'll bring it to you, and the final decision will be yours. But let me do this for you. I found the cow."

"The cow?"

I kissed her lightly. "I'll explain it to you someday. Or have my father explain it. Either way, just say yes."

She searched my face. "Without knowing what I'm saying yes to?"

"Everything worthwhile in life is a risk, Wren. I'm asking you to take a leap of faith. Let me do this. Let me bring you and your father a truly genius surprise."

"Genius, huh?" She wrinkled her nose, then chuckled. "I do trust you, Mauricio. So yes—yes to whatever the hell you're talking about."

I kissed her then, the brief, respectful kind of kiss a man sneaks with the woman he loves at the home of his parents. Then I called out, "You can all come back in now."

They came out of the kitchen, each holding something for the table as if they'd all left the room for that purpose.

Christof looked from me to Wren and back. "So are we celebrating anything?"

Smiling, Wren threw her hands up in the air. "Mauricio is getting me a cow."

My father hugged my mother. "That's my boy."

"I don't understand," Christof said.

Gian shrugged. "I don't either."

Sebastian nodded. "Tell me if there is any way I can help, Mauricio."

Wren turned to Heather. "Do you know what they're talking about?"

Heather shook her head but wrapped an arm around her husband. "No, but if these men are planning it, it's going to be wonderful."

Ava stepped forward. "I love cows. Uncle Mauricio, can you get me a cow too? My pony would love one."

We all laughed, which confused her. She clarified, "I'm serious. Why are you all laughing?"

Which only made it funnier, but we all did our best to not offend her by laughing more.

Thankfully, we had an easily available distraction—homemade cookies.

I picked one up, offered it to Ava, and just like that she forgave us.

CHAPTER THIRTY-THREE

WREN

A month later, in a small town in Iowa, Mauricio held open a door of a breakfast place. We'd flown out on his plane, driven straight there from the airport, and although he was grinning from ear to ear, he had yet to tell me why.

I didn't push, because I would have followed him anywhere. If meeting his family hadn't confirmed my feelings for him, when I'd seen him with mine I was all his. Mauricio claimed to be universally likable. I laughed whenever he said it, until I brought him over to eat with my family, and afterward he'd asked my father if he knew how to play canasta. "My only suggestion is that the men are on one team and the women on the other. I can get unruly if my canasta partner goes out while I'm still hoarding points in my hand."

My father's eyebrows had risen. "Canasta. Isn't that a game for the old?"

"You're no spring chicken, sir," Mauricio had said with a straight face.

It was the first time I'd seen my father laugh at anything a date of mine had said. They'd tossed little barbs back and forth for the next hour or so while my mom and I kicked their butts at cards. By the end, I could tell my father approved of Mauricio.

My mother was equally sold on him when he cleared the table even after she told him he didn't need to. I warned her not to be fooled by his good behavior and ratted him out for taunting his family until they tossed food at him.

Both of my parents loved the scene I'd painted—and suddenly everything I'd worried about didn't matter as much. I was a little confused a couple of weeks later, when I told Mauricio I had gotten an interview with a local electric company, and he asked me not to take the position. He asked for a little more time to work the kinks out of his project.

It was indeed a leap of faith, but I waited. I lived off my savings and trusted he wouldn't ask me to if he didn't have a good reason. Waiting required more trust than I had for other people, but this was Mauricio.

And, yes, a steady supply of great sex was giving me a Zen-like view of the world. It would all turn out the way it was meant to.

Eight, by the way. I'd learned I could orgasm eight times in one day before my brain turned to mush. The morning after our first night I'd stayed at his place in the US, he'd woken me with a gift. In true Mauricio fashion, he'd gone down on one knee, held the box out, and said, "Cinderella, I believe you left this at the ball. Do you mind if I see if it fits?"

I'd guessed at the contents even before I'd opened the box. "What they say is true—we'll always have Paris." My vibrator, that is. The name fit it perfectly.

So yes, my limit was eight, but we had so much fun testing that number. Again and again. Mauricio was a little competitive, even when it was against his own record.

I didn't mind that.

I'm the same way. After a little side reading, I'd brought a few tricks of my own to our lovemaking. I don't want to brag, but thanks to me, he has also exceeded his personal record. Sadly, that was only four. Still working on it.

Now, in Iowa, we followed a young woman across the restaurant, and I took a moment to study the photos on the wall. "The king of Vandorra comes here? How cool is that?"

Mauricio winked at me. "You wouldn't think this town would have enough to lure royalty, would you? Never judge a book by its cover. Take me, for example. I bet when you met me, you thought I was just a good-looking man with perfectly sculpted abs."

It was a joke that revealed the many layers of the man I loved. On one hand, some people saw him only in terms of the superficial, and it bothered him. On the other hand, all that attention had given him an ego robust enough that thankfully he could also poke fun at himself. I loved all his layers, even the ones that sometimes required a trim, so I hip checked him and gave his hard-as-rock stomach a pat. "Careful. They say love puts pounds on a person."

He looked down at me in dismay, then smiled. "Well, we'll have to keep thinking of new exercises, won't we?"

That was another layer I loved—he was so open with how he felt about me. No games. No pressure to be anyone but myself with him. I went on my tiptoes and suggested something for the plane ride home. His cheeks flushed, and his eyes lit with desire. Love with Mauricio was easy.

We sat down at a booth. An older woman came over, introduced herself as Lily, and placed a cup of coffee in front of each of us. "Good to see you again, Mauricio. Bryant and Nicolette will be here in a few. Don't let all the waitstaff make you lazy. You want more coffee? The pot is right over there."

"Yes, ma'am," Mauricio said with a smile.

Lily looked me over. I held out my hand to her. "Wren Heath."

She shook my hand, then nodded toward Mauricio. "It'll take a strong woman to keep a man like that in line."

I cracked my knuckles and shot Mauricio a look. "I believe I have what it takes."

He winked at Lily. "I fear her wrath."

Lily laughed. "You picked a good one, Mauricio." She turned at the sound of the door opening. "Here's Bryant and Nicolette now." She wandered off to meet them.

I leaned toward Mauricio and in a low voice asked, "Bryant?"

In an equally discreet tone, Mauricio answered, "Bryant Taunton. He's the industry leader in robotics integration into the health field. I wanted you two to meet before I tossed him my proposal."

My heart was doing a crazy beat in my chest. This was his surprise? He was getting me a job in Iowa? *No. No. No. He knows I can't leave my family.* I met Mauricio's gaze and my doubt fell away. *Wait. He knows all that. This has to be about something else. He asked me to trust him, and I do.* "So meeting him is your surprise?"

"Part of it."

We stood to greet Bryant and his wife. Hugs all around. They were about our age, and the friendship between Mauricio and Bryant seemed to be a comfortable one.

Introductions over, we all sat in the booth. This time, Mauricio took the spot beside me. He gave my leg a pat beneath the table. "Bryant, this isn't just a social visit. I'd like you to meet an engineer who is about to change the world of prosthetics."

"You are?" Bryant asked with real interest.

I swallowed hard. This was the first I'd heard of it, but it was a dream I had to hear only once to realize how well it fit. "My father refuses to wear the ones the VA provides for him. There are more advanced models out there, but they aren't affordable, not the ones that could do what he'd need them to do, anyway." As I spoke, my confidence soared. "I could change that."

Mauricio took out his phone and went into his mail. "I've spent the last month looking into what it would take to make that happen. We're based on the East Coast. I have investors ready and a satellite site out there. We have a dialogue with the biomedical department at Johns

Hopkins regarding collaboration. What I'd like from you is confirmation that if we come up with a viable prototype, you'd be open to at least consider mass manufacturing it."

My gaze flew to meet Mauricio's. "You have investors? Already? I don't even have a design."

He took my hand in his. "You believed in me. I have faith in you, Wren. Besides, Felix owed me a favor, and his father is actually impressed with his initiative to invest more into US businesses."

"Felix is on board?" Bryant asked. "Then you know I'm in. Bring me something good, though. You know me. It has to be high quality, patient based, and AI integrable. Impress me and we'll talk contracts. How much time are you looking at from design to prototype?"

They all turned to me. There was a time when that kind of pressure would have stolen my ability to breathe, but not with Mauricio at my side. Together I knew we could do this. "Six months to a year. I won't bring you anything before we've field-tested it."

We. I was still getting used to thinking like that.

Even as I was reeling from the unexpectedness of Mauricio's surprise, I trusted it would work out, because this was what Mauricio did—he saw what people needed and he stepped in to help them reach their dreams. People relied on him because they knew he not only had a good head for business but also wanted the best for those around him.

Sebastian had shared with me how much of a role Mauricio had played in the success of their family business. Since Paris, Felix had reached out and thanked Mauricio for always cheering him on. Helping me move forward with a dream I'd lost faith in, one that allowed me to help my father while creating something that would make a positive impact in the world . . . I shouldn't have been surprised by the move at all. Luckily I had the rest of my life to find ways to make him as happy as he'd made me.

Bryant nodded. "I like her."

Nicolette hugged Bryant's arm. "It's nice to see you with someone, Mauricio."

Mauricio tucked me to his side. "I couldn't let Bryant be the only happy one in our crew."

After that, business was put aside, and the two men entertained Nicolette and me with stories of when they were younger and wilder. They playfully tried to one-up each other until we were all laughing and calling bullshit.

We toured Bryant's factory, where I was delighted to meet Jordan Cohen, a man who had become a household name for his work in VR but had partnered with Bryant on medical applications of his programs. "I'm a huge fan," I said while vigorously shaking his hand. "I have your photo app on my phone."

His wife, Paisley, laughed. "Which one? Tell me it's not the bikini one."

"No. I'm addicted to the one that automatically catalogs photos from various digital sources, then makes them voice searchable. It's freaky to watch it in action, but pure genius."

Jordan smiled down at his wife. "You hear that? *Genius.*"

She chuckled. "He loves that word. You've made his day."

They were so comfortable to talk to, I said, "I hope I'm able to bring something equally amazing to the table."

"You will." He hugged his wife closer. "Just make sure you surround yourself with people who believe in you, and anything is possible."

I leaned into Mauricio's embrace. "I've got that part covered."

CHAPTER THIRTY-FOUR

MAURICIO

Early the next afternoon, Wren and I went to see her parents. With the sun out and a cool breeze blowing, we gathered on their front porch.

"How was Iowa?" her mother asked as soon as we all settled onto the wicker furniture.

I looked to Wren to answer. To me, it had gone even better than expected. We'd spent the day with my friends, stayed overnight at Bryant and Nicolette's home, and come home with smiles on our faces that morning. Still, I wanted to hear how Wren described it.

"It was amazing. I'll tell you all about it, but first I have a question for Dad." Wren folded and unfolded her hands. I laid my hand over them in support. She shot me a grateful smile.

"What do you want to know, baby?" her father asked.

She took a breath as if gathering her courage. "Why don't you wear a prosthetic arm?"

Her father shrugged. "We've talked about this. You know none of the ones at the VA do what I'd want them to do."

Wren persisted. "What would you want one to do? Specifically? If you could have any kind of arm, how would you imagine it?"

Her father looked at me, his expression closing as he did. "I appreciate the thought, but I wouldn't feel comfortable accepting something like that from anyone—not even you. I do just fine like I am."

Once again, I deferred to Wren. I knew it was important for her to make this connection with her father.

"Mauricio isn't offering to buy you one, Dad. He and I are going to design one. So I need to know what would be most useful to you."

My mother exclaimed, "I love the idea of the two of you working on a project together."

"Mauricio found investors, and we've connected with Johns Hopkins for crowdsourcing ideas. We have leads as far as production. What we need to do now is to narrow down what to focus on. There are already a lot of prosthetic options out there. I don't want to re-create what they're doing. My goal is to have something that is affordable, high tech, useful, and upgradable. If you could have whatever you wanted, Dad, what would you want?"

There was such hope in Wren's eyes. I wished her father had immediately loved the idea. He was silent, his expression indiscernible. "Nothing will ever be as good as what I lost," he said.

And my heart sank a little.

Wren stood and walked over to where her father was sitting. I could almost see the wheels turning in her head, and I'd never wanted anyone to succeed as much as I wanted her to reach her father right then. "I'm doing this, Dad. With or without you. I'm going to create something that will help injured soldiers get their lives back. You can help me or you can sit there feeling sorry for yourself and watch me do it on my own."

Her father's chin rose. His eyes went dark with emotion.

She continued, "I've never done anything like this before. I'm not going to lie, Dad. I'm scared, but that's not going to stop me. I've always been better than you at coming up with ideas . . ." She went down on her knees before him. "But you've always been better than I am at seeing why something doesn't work."

He looked from her face to mine, then back. His face tightened, and for a moment I wasn't sure he could beat the sadness in his eyes. "I'm not the man I once was."

Wren nodded and shed a tear for him. "That's what I'm counting on. This is a second chance for both of us. Mauricio helped me see I was letting fear of failing hold me back from reaching my dreams. Reach with me. I need you, Dad. Help me do this."

He leaned down and hugged her, closing his eyes as he did. "Oh, baby, I don't know if I can."

Wren glanced back at me with love in her eyes before turning back to him. "I believe in you. I know it's scary, but take a leap of faith with me . . . with us. Let's design something together that makes a difference." She glanced back at me again. "All of us. Together."

Her father helped her to her feet; then in a gruff tone he said, "The hand part should be detachable. Realistic with fingers is nice, but I'd want more practical options as well. Give me the ability to use it as a tool, to easily change out which attachment I'm using. Bluetooth isn't a bad idea, either, while we're brainstorming."

"Bluetooth," I echoed. "I like that. We'll be integrating it with AI, so that would be a natural extension. Essentially we could put a micro-computer inside. People have already developed the technology to have a hand respond to upper-arm movements. It would need sensors and a power source."

Wren came back to sit with me. She looked excited now. "It can't cost more than a cell phone."

"It also needs a light. I hate hearing your father stumbling around in the dark," my mother added.

"If we connect it to the internet, I could get recipes while I'm cooking," her father said, a smile beginning to spread across his face.

Wren nodded. "Let's write everything down, then see how much of it is possible. We need to keep it durable as well."

Her father was nodding again. "I can imagine what I want in my head. If you're serious about me working on this with you, I can hire some more help for the gas station."

"Oh my God, yes, Dad."

Wren and I exchanged a look. I knew exactly what this meant to her, and being a part of why it was happening was a feeling I would always remember. It was a moment so intense, I had to add, "Now on to something more important." I took a ring box out of my pocket and bounced it in my hand. "I'm getting ready to ask Wren to marry me. Before I do, could someone please tell me if she knows how to cook?"

Wren's father barked out a laugh.

Her mother took out her phone to FaceTime with my parents. "This is it, Camilla. He's about to ask."

"Wait for Dad," my mother called out. "He's coming. Okay. He's here. Go ahead, Mauricio."

I looked over at Wren's father. "I want to ask your permission, but . . ."

He smiled at me. "She'd kick your ass for implying either of us held the outdated impression that I have some kind of ownership of her and could transfer that over to you."

"But we both know that it's really a respect thing between you and me." He nodded and I continued, "So this is me not asking."

His eyes were twinkling. "This is me not saying I wholeheartedly approve."

Wren wagged a finger at both of us. "Saying you are not doing something while you are doesn't change what you're doing."

"Just ask her, son, then let's go out to dinner with your parents to celebrate," her father said with a chuckle.

I liked the sound of that.

I dropped down on one knee in front of Wren and opened the ring box. I'd chosen something simple, built solid, like I wanted our marriage to be. "Wren Heath, marry me. Let's build a business together, buy a big house, fill it with five kids, and live happily ever after with two dogs and maybe a cat. I'm not sure about the cat. I know kids like them, but they're a little uppity to me."

She laughed and slid her finger into the ring. "We'll figure the cat thing out later. I would love to marry you. Yes."

"She said yes," my mother said in an excited tone.

"I can hear," my father joked.

I stood, spun Wren in my arms, and kissed her. She wrapped her arms around my neck. It was a brief kiss, but one I would never forget.

That's my future wife—right there.

My mother chimed in, "Don't forget to call Nonna. You should plan to go see her too. Sebastian did after he got engaged."

I looked down at Wren. "We did France. Are you up for Italy? I haven't seen her in years."

"Absolutely. I remember what you said she did with Sebastian. Nonna needs to know you're off the market," she joked.

CHAPTER THIRTY-FIVE

WREN

International flight was entirely different in a private plane. Amazing how a little champagne and a bedroom with a door made a flight zip by like nothing. We were dressed again and seat belted in and readied to land at a private airport near Montalcino, Italy, when the pilot came on and said we'd been asked to divert to a larger airport. The plane would circle as he requested information regarding why.

"I've never had that happen," Mauricio said, looking out the window. I did as well. We couldn't see anything through the low-lying clouds.

The pilot came back on the intercom. "Looks like the airport has a VIP who requested all runways close until he takes off. I exaggerated our fuel situation, and they said they'd speak to him about letting us land on a small runway on the side."

Mauricio frowned and stood, walking over to the cockpit. I went with him. It was rare to see Mauricio irritated. "Tell them we're landing. I don't know what asshole would require a plane that was low on fuel to wait, but unless they're prepared to shoot us down—we're landing."

I've never been afraid of flying, but I've also never landed when told not to. "We have the fuel to divert, though, right? I don't care if it takes us a little longer to get there. Isn't there a commercial airport nearby?"

Mauricio shook his head. "I'm a nice guy, Wren, but if I have a button, it's people who think having money means they're more important than everyone else. Whoever is down there feels he or she is entitled to inconvenience us without thought about who we are or what we're doing here. We're landing."

The pilot spoke to the ground control, then turned to say, "We've just been given clearance to, but they said only on the side runway. It's Dominic Corisi, and apparently he travels with a security team that secures the area as part of their protocol."

"Dominic Corisi," I said, instantly recognizing the name of a man known for dominating the tech industry and becoming one of the richest people in the world by breaking into the Chinese market. He and his wife were reclusive. There should have been much more about him in the news, but people said he was that powerful—so powerful that in an age of everything ending up online, his family had a very limited presence. I touched Mauricio's arm. "That's kind of cool, right? Maybe we'll catch a glimpse of him."

Mauricio didn't look pleased, but by the time we'd returned to our seats, he was smiling again. "So what are you most excited about this trip?"

I laced my fingers through his. "Nonna's ravioli. I need to see if it lives up to the hype."

"Oh, it will."

"And meeting your cousins. I've been practicing some Italian, but beyond asking for the bathroom, I'm not sure how well I'll do."

"They speak English. My Italian is horrible. I haven't seen them in years, but if I remember right, we'll all be drinking so much we'll feel like we understand them. They make their own wine." He grinned at me. "They're going to love you right after they initially hate you for not being Italian."

I laughed. "That's reassuring."

"It's a tight community. My mother said they take care of their own. When Gian first came to us, I heard Mom talking on the phone to her sister, Gian's mother. I was young, so I might have gotten it wrong, but I thought she'd said she wanted him to be raised with family rather than on the run. It sounded like a witness protection program or something. I tried to ask my mother about it later, but she doesn't talk about her sister. Years later, I asked Nonna about what I'd heard. She said she only had one daughter. I told her I knew that wasn't true—Gian's biological mother was her daughter. She said her other daughter was dead to her. I'm only telling you this because I don't talk about Gian when I'm here. It makes Nonna sad."

"Of course. I won't bring him up."

"That's what I do. It's sad, though, because I know Gian would like to come here, but none of us want to risk that it might not go well. His bio parents must have been real prizes. Or maybe mob informants. I really have no idea."

I nodded in understanding and held his hand. We touched down, and the topic naturally came to an end. After gathering up our things, we stepped out onto the plane's stairway. There were enough black SUVs and security for a presidential visit. I smacked Mauricio's arm when I spotted a man in a dark suit making his way toward the plane. He had jet-black hair. "I bet that's Dominic Corisi," I exclaimed.

The man turned in our direction as if he'd heard me, even though he was too far away to. "Oh my God, doesn't he look just like Sebastian? They could be twins."

Mauricio dismissed my observation and led the way down the steps. He walked up to the nearest security guard and said, "My name is Mauricio Romano. Tell Mr. Corisi I'd like to have a word with him before he leaves."

"He doesn't do autographs," the guard said with a closed expression, then walked away.

I put my hand on Mauricio's arm. "Come on. Forget about him. He doesn't matter."

Mauricio's expression warmed as he looked down at me. "You're right. I'm sorry. This trip is about us and family. I wanted to tell him he should show a little more consideration for fellow fliers, but he's probably a miserable prick who wouldn't care anyway."

I touched Mauricio's cheek and mimicked how a mother would talk to a child. "Oh, did poor little Mauricio almost have to wait to land his plane?"

His grin returned in full force. "I'm not that bad."

I went up on my toes and kissed his lips. "You're exactly that bad, but I love you anyway. Forget about him and let's go see Nonna."

He laughed and pulled me full against him. He kissed me deeply, then said, "Forget about who? Where are we? You're dangerously capable of wiping everything else from my brain."

There was so much I could have said. I was so happy I could have started every day by thanking him for showing me love could be fun and still be responsible. I could have listed all the ways he made my life better and gotten teary just by thinking that I still wanted to pinch myself every time I pictured forever with him at my side.

Yes, life could be that good and be real.

Instead I took a page from his book, batted my eyelashes at him, and said, "I know. Now shut up and kiss me."

He did, and I discovered that I loved Italy as much as I'd loved France. Wherever Mauricio and I were was now my favorite place.

CHAPTER THIRTY-SIX

DOMINIC

Dominic Corisi downed a shot of scotch as soon as he boarded his plane. Before sitting down, he poured himself a second and downed that as well.

He wasn't a drinker—hadn't been for a very long time. He needed something, though, to take the edge off his rage.

Everything he'd achieved, even the peace he'd finally come to with his past, had been swept away as soon as the first door had slammed in his face. He hadn't needed to say his last name; everyone in Montalcino recognized him.

He remembered this feeling all too clearly, this absolute rejection. His prior visits there were burned into his memories. He'd told himself they'd been able to hurt him only because he'd been young and desperate. A younger him had begged everyone who'd made time to meet him—begged them for information about where his mother was.

He had his mother back in his life now. He didn't need their help anymore.

And still—their refusal to talk to him cut him to the core. His own grandmother had refused to meet with him.

Like I'm no one.

Like they didn't hurt my family as much as my father did.

A dark anger, one he'd thought he'd conquered long ago, took hold of his heart. As his plane took off, he called the one person he knew could get him what he wanted. "Alethea," he growled into the phone, "I want you to go to Montalcino. Dig up every secret that town has. I don't care what you have to do. Bring me leverage on every damn person there. They will never say no to me again."

ACKNOWLEDGMENTS

I am so grateful to everyone who was part of the process of creating *The Wild One.*

Thank you to:

Montlake Romance, for giving Dominic a chance to find his family. Special thanks to Lauren Plude for encouraging me each step of the way.

My very patient beta readers. You know who you are. Thank you for kicking my butt when I need it.

My editors: Karen Lawson, Janet Hitchcock, and Krista Stroever. As well as all the talented line editors who polished away my mistakes.

My Roadies, for making me smile each day when I log on to my computer. So many of you have become friends. Was there life before the Roadies? I'm sure there was, but it wasn't as much fun.

Thank you to my husband, Tony, who is a saint—simple as that.

And my children, who have given me so many wonderful memories. I hope my love for them shines through in every story I write.

ABOUT THE AUTHOR

Ruth Cardello is the *New York Times* bestselling author of the Westerly Billionaire novels and *The Broken One* in the Corisi Billionaires series. She loves writing about rich alpha men and the strong women who tame them. Before becoming a novelist, Ruth was an educator for two decades, including eleven years as a kindergarten teacher. Born the youngest of eleven children in a small city in northern Rhode Island, Ruth has lived in Boston, Paris, Orlando, New York, and Rhode Island again before moving to Massachusetts, where she now lives with her husband and three children. Learn about Ruth at www.RuthCardello.com.